Hearts in the Spotlight

Happy Reading
Katie Oh!

ALSO BY KATIE O'CONNOR

Contemporary Romance Series

Heart's Haven (Resplendence Publishing)

Running Home

Saving Grace

Building Trust

Contemporary Romance Single Title

To a Tea

Rekindled Fire

Erotic Romance/Erotica

Stand Alone Erotic Romances

Tessa's Trio

The Gift

Covet the Cowboy Erotic Romance Series

Corralling the Cowboy (Book 1)

Cornering the Cowgirl (Book 2)

Hearts in the Spotlight

A WOMEN OF STAMPEDE NOVEL

KATIE O'CONNOR

SNARKY HEART PRESS

—Hearts in the Spotlight—
This book is a work of fiction. Names, characters, places, and incidents either are products of the author's imagination or are used fictitiously. Any resemblance to actual events, locales, or persons, living or dead, is entirely coincidental.

Copyright © 2018 by Katie O'Connor
All rights reserved. No part of this book may be reproduced in any form or by any electronic or mechanical means including information storage and retrieval systems, except in the case of brief quotations embodied in critical articles or reviews, without permission in writing from its copyright holder.

Published May 2018 by Snarky Heart Press and Katie O'Connor
(katieohwrites.com)

ISBN: 978-1-7752233-4-4 (Print edition)

Design and cover art by Su Kopil, Earthly Charms
Copyediting by Ted Williams

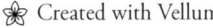 Created with Vellum

DEDICATION

This book, *Hearts in the Spotlight*, my tenth published story, is dedicated to the hard working, supportive staff of Ronald McDonald House Children's Charity.

When my first grandchild was born, she had a heart defect and required open heart and tracheal surgery. The fabulous staff at the Stollery Children's Hospital in Edmonton helped us through this event. During her month-long stay at the hospital, her mother, father and I were privileged and blessed to stay at RMH in Edmonton. For those not familiar with this fabulous organization, they provide housing to families whose children are in the hospital enabling them to be close to their loved ones during stressful times.

With beds, private rooms and meals provided, RMH helped us survive and gave us a safe, welcoming place to stay and to unwind. It was our home away from home. We cannot thank the house staff and the people who donate their time and money to this worthy charity enough. My lovely granddaughter survived the surgery and has blossomed.

A portion of the proceeds from the sale of this book are being donated to Ronald McDonald House. The funds will be split between the Edmonton location where we stayed and our hometown location in Calgary.

Hearts in the Spotlight is also dedicated to my friends and fans who worked with me in plotting Brett and Stephanie's story and naming the characters. This one's for you: Mandy Eve Barnett, Terri St. Clair, Jean Anne, Deb Isaac, Samantha Talarico, Jenna Harte, and Andrea Corbin.

FOREWORD

Hearts in the Spotlight, as written by my colleague and close friend, Katie O'Connor, illuminates the song or winsome ballad that Brett Wyatt and Steph Alexander explore from the opening passages to the happily ever after conclusion. It seems a fitting title for a novel that squeezes a reader's heartstrings, reaching inside her chest, almost forcing the cessation of breath. It gripped me.

As a past singer, I've had moments in the spotlight when my vocal cords cracked, or my singing voice slipped away, so the moments where the hero and heroine struggle with the threat of losing a natural talent, *really* touched me.

I beta-read this book, pleading with the author inside the novel's sidelines, to give a fictional character hope. A voice. A song. A career.

I cried. I'm crying now… remembering.

This is a work of Romance. A story I feel privileged to have read.

Shelley Kassian, the author of the Women of Stampede novel, *The Half Mile of Baby Blue.*

AUTHOR'S NOTE

The Calgary Stampede was a huge part of my life for many years. Throughout my thirties, I was part of a theatrical group known as Guns of the Golden West. We dressed in late 1800s costumes and performed mock gunfights year round.

During the busy Stampede season, we put on anywhere from five to fifteen shows a day around Calgary and three or four daily shows in Weadickville, a mock western town situated on the Stampede Grounds and dedicated to one of the Calgary Stampede founders, Guy Weadick.

From these performances, and my immersion in western life, past and present, my love of this annual event blossomed. I adore everything from the nightly Grandstand Show to the agricultural displays. Cotton candy, corn dogs, beer tents, concerts and midway rides help round out this ten-day extravaganza.

Having been a Winter Carnival queen in my youth, I have a special place in my heart for those young girls who put their self-confidence on the line and compete for the title of queen. It isn't as easy as you think. It takes a tough heart and brave soul to learn public speaking and answer questions you're totally unprepared for. And, let's not forget the endless public appearances, having a

AUTHOR'S NOTE

stranger pick your clothing, and smiling 24/7 until you feel like your face will freeze that way. Still, it wasn't all bad. I met some great people and made lifelong friends while I developed numerous life skills. I came out a braver woman for the trials.

Hearts in the Spotlight and Women of Stampede is my way of sharing my joy and fascination with rodeo and the Stampede with my readers.

ACKNOWLEDGMENTS

Thanks to Ted Williams for line editing and Su Kopil for the fabulous cover.

Special thanks to Shelley Kassian, Brenda Sinclair, Kara Leigh Miller, and Terri St. Clair for critiquing my work and pointing out flaws and plot holes. Any remaining mistakes are my own.

Kudos to the authors in this group for putting up with my shenanigans, the timing shifts and occasional short temper. You girls rock!

Without the assistance of this fabulous group this book wouldn't exist.

CHAPTER 1

*B*rett Wyatt climbed out of his rented pickup and stretched his back. Five hours of non-stop driving meant kinks and discomfort. But he'd made it alive; without falling asleep on the road. Lady Luck was with him today. Now if luck held, he'd be able to perform his three shows during the Calgary Stampede without his voice acting up.

He could hardly believe his manager had arranged three consecutive concerts. One at the Saddledome, one at Deerfoot Inn and Casino and the third on Stampede grounds on the Coca-Cola Stage. It was a darn good thing he had three weeks to rest up first. Non-stop touring and performances were wearing him down and wreaking havoc with his voice.

A sprawling, white, two-story house stood before him. A discreet sign indicated this was, indeed, The Wild Rose Inn. Wild Alberta rose bushes lined the front walkway, their branches laden with pink blooms from the tiniest bud to the fullest flower; their simple five-petal blossoms in shades from pinky-white to almost fuchsia. His grandmother would have loved them.

Navy blue shutters framed the windows. The same blue paint topped the white railings of the wrap around porch. Baskets of trailing flowers hung from the eaves and stood on the floor and pillars in a wild array of colors. Cozy swings and comfortable-looking chairs were scattered across the porch, inviting him to sit and rest. His body yearned to drop onto a swing and take a nap. First, he needed to check in and unload his bags and guitar.

He winced as he approached the front porch of the B&B he'd reserved for the three weeks between now and Stampede. Off-key singing grated his guitar-string-tight nerves making his left eye twitch. After eight months of continuous touring he was ready for a nice quiet vacation. No fans, no stress, nothing to do but sit outdoors and read a good book; or if he felt like it, compose a new song.

Composing was an issue. Maybe it was just exhaustion, but something was hindering his muse. He'd written exactly two songs in the past year and they were shit. Complete and total crap. Three-year-old kids wrote better music. And the lyrics? He shuddered just thinking about them. His recording label was clamoring for a new album and if he didn't produce one soon, they'd cut his contract and his touring days would be over. Life was nothing without music. Just thinking about it almost paralyzed him with fear.

Resting his body and his voice was why he was here, at this rural bed and breakfast. He needed to relax and unwind. His best friend, Tucker, promised this was the perfect place for Brett's needs, but the screeching coming from inside said otherwise. He mounted the three steps, passed a wide-eye Shepherd-lab cross lazing in the sun, and crossed the pristine white porch in two quick strides. The hand he'd raised to knock dropped uselessly to his side as he stared in disbelief at the gyrating woman in front of him, just inside the screen door. Caught up in the music, *his music*, she pivoted, twirled and belted out the worst mockery he'd ever heard of his latest hit song. She had the words entirely wrong, was singing it from a woman's perspective, not a man's; and she was completely and totally tone deaf. She sounded like a cat stuck in a wringer washer. But, hot damn, could she move!

In his younger days, before he'd hit it big on the country music circuit, he'd visited a strip bar or two; but this woman, whoever she was, could out-dance most pros. She toyed with the broom in her hands like it was a pole, spinning and gyrating around it. Her waist-length auburn hair shimmered and swayed against her back, just tickling the top of the most curvaceous and kissable ass he'd seen in weeks. Hell, in years; and lord knows he saw a lot of backsides. Groupies flung themselves at him in droves after every concert. Why couldn't they just enjoy his music and respect him as a human? He was more than a body and a voice.

Guilt niggled at his conscience. Wasn't that just a case of the pot calling the kettle black? He was ogling her and whining about being treated as a sex object. Hypocrisy much? The thought stuttered to a halt when she spun around to face the door. Dear God! Long dark lashes lay on her porcelain cheeks, her mouth opened in a round 'oh' as she belted out yet another off-key phrase. But her mouth—pretty, pink lips begged to be kissed and he knew just the man to do it. Him. Nobody should kiss that mouth except him.

She wasn't tall, nor was she short. Maybe five-foot six and she was fit and toned, those tight denim shorts and cropped T-shirt hid nothing. Not her narrow waist, luscious hips or breasts the perfect size to fit in his hands. Geez, she was a wet dream incarnate.

He could interrupt her, clear his throat and let her know he was here. A gentleman would announce his presence. Naw, that was *so* not going to happen.

She pivoted, twisted and swung her hips back and forth like she was grinding her way down a man's body and all the way back up again. He tugged his suddenly tight collar and shifted to ease the tightness in his jeans. He had to end this. Now. Before he had an even worse physical reaction. He winced at another screeching note as she neared the chorus. He drew in a deep breath, opened his mouth and joined in.

∼

This had to be her favorite song of all time. The entire CD was gold. She'd downloaded it onto her phone, her computer, her MP3 player. Wherever she went, Brett Wyatt's sexy, soothing voice was right there with her. She must have played his latest disc a hundred times. She knew the lyrics by heart, well most of them; she stumbled on occasion, but nobody was around to hear it, so who cared?

She'd love to see Brett in concert again but hadn't been able to work up the courage to buy tickets. He was an enormous celebrity, and the media would be all over his events. Lord knew she hated the spotlight; so, she'd miss the concert and avoid the risk of being recognized. Listening to his music at home would have to suffice. Maybe someday she'd work up the courage to attend another show; but not this time.

She should be cleaning, she had a full booking for the next three weeks. Some enormous, faceless corporation had booked her entire B&B for a retreat. All six individual rooms in the main house and all ten rooms in the bunkhouse. She'd had to hire extra staff, but the money they'd offered had been irresistible. She wasn't avaricious by nature, but damn. Who could resist? She'd make enough off this group that she might even be able to close for a few days and take a vacation—if she worked up the courage to leave her sanctuary and head into the public eye.

She belted out another line of lyrics. Yeah, she should be getting ready for guests, but they weren't due to arrive for hours and all she had left to do was finish sweeping, mop the floor and prepare for supper. With her bestie, Penny, doing most of the cooking, she had tons of time to enjoy herself. She was happy and depression-free for the first time in months and she was going to enjoy herself.

Now for the chorus.

As she belted out lyrics, the volume of the singer amped up; it was like she was singing along with Brett Wyatt himself, though he'd probably cringe at her awful rendition. Meh. Who cared? She loved this song. She jacked her voice up to match the weirdly increased vocals.

Whoa!

Wait. She was home alone. Nobody else here to jack up the volume. Her eyes flew open, she stumbled to a halt and stared slack-jawed at the man standing outside the screen door on her front porch. Holy-Mary-Mother-of-God. Backlit by the sun, the mystery singer was barely more than a silhouette. Even so, he was every girl's fantasy. Clinging, faded denim jeans, a tight T-shirt, cowboy hat pulled low over his eyes and a singing voice like sin. Damned if he didn't sound just like Brett Wyatt.

Oh no! Hell no!

She'd been booked by B.W. Enterprises. It couldn't be. She closed her eyes and his velvet voice stroked over her skin like a fantasy. Even unassisted by editing and sound-board tweaking, she knew that voice. Fudge! It was him. She opened her eyes and blinked stupidly at him.

"Can I help you?" She meant to sound polite and accommodating, but the words grated out like an accusation. Oh great, that's the way to make a good impression.

"Hi. I've got a booking for today." His sexy singing turned into muted laughter.

Fudge. Fudge. Fudge and strawberry shortcake, too.

"B.W. Enterprises?" Dear God, tell her she hadn't booked her B&B out to the hottest country sensation in a decade. She'd been fantasizing about him since she saw him in concert two years ago, since before her life turned to crap and she'd retreated to her grandparents' ranch and turned it into a B&B. Brett Wyatt was not on her front porch and he hadn't just caught her murdering one of his songs. Had he?

"In the flesh." He opened the old-fashioned, wooden screen door, stepped through and offered his hand. "I'm…"

Don't say it. Oh, sweet heaven, don't say it. The words ran prayer-like over and over in her head in the scant seconds it took him to finish his sentence.

"Brett Wyatt."

Her shoulders slumped, so much for good luck. His laughing gaze threatened to torch her alive. Hell's bells. A deep, long-forgotten longing surfaced. Maybe she wasn't as happy single as she thought she was.

"Welcome to the Wild Rose Inn. I'm Stephanie Alexander. Call me Steph." She eyed his hand warily before finally accepting it. Dang it, even his hands were sexy. Strong, tanned, work-roughened, she just couldn't catch a break here. Bolts of heat sparked up her forearm and she jerked her hand back and stared at his. Oh man, she had to stop staring like a ninny. He'd think she was a nutcase.

Where had those sparks come from?

"What the…?" Great, she couldn't even form a coherent sentence in front of a superstar musician. The next three weeks were going to be an agonizing disaster of blushing, stammering and stumbling about if she didn't get a grip on herself.

"That's what I'd like to know. You, Stephanie Alexander, pack one hell of a punch."

"Must be the dry air." Yeah, like he'd buy such a pathetic excuse. Whoa! She packed a punch? He must have felt it, too; maybe it *was* the air. You know, static electricity and all that.

"Dry air?" He raised one eyebrow and the left corner of his lips turned up in a mocking grin, his deep blue eyes sparkling with mirth. "Lady, Steph, except for the driveway, your yard is a mud pit. It looks like it's been raining for a week. I thought they claimed it never rained during Stampede week."

"It doesn't. Well, rarely anyway. The city gets the odd storm and a bit of weather, but Mother Nature doesn't often dump a deluge of water on the Stampede. Besides, it's weeks until Stampede. You should know, you're headlining this year. By then, the weather will be perfect, watch and see." His half-smile broke into a full-blown grin and he chuckled.

He was killing her. She was killing herself. She couldn't even think straight. Brett Wyatt was in her entryway. Here. At the Wild

Rose Inn. Now. And she'd been massacring his latest hit song. Life just didn't get any worse than this.

"Yeah, sorry about the singing." She steadfastly ignored the heat in her cheeks. His deep chuckle trembled across her skin and into the pit of her stomach. Oh yeah, she was done for. He'd never stay now. So much for a full-booking windfall.

"Your singing was—"

"Agonizing, brutal, hideous, heinous…should I go on?" She winced and stared at the floor, thinking about her altered version.

"It was unique and enthusiastic." His belly laugh relaxed her. "I admit, I've never heard it sung quite that way."

Her gaze flew to his face. Damned if he wasn't smiling his patented, come-hither, sex on a stick grin; the one gracing all his posters. Including the one on the back of her bedroom door. Her insides melted, just a little. Oh no! She was not going to fall into those gorgeous blue eyes with lashes women would kill for. Heck no. Not now, not ever. She didn't need him here. Okay, maybe her bank balance needed him, but her traitorous body did not, and she wasn't falling for his country charm, either. She might have been raised in a small town, but she knew a big city wolf when she saw one. And Brett Wyatt was all big city sexuality and masculinity. Dude probably got his muscles from the gym, not real work.

"Come on in, Mr. Wyatt. We'll get you checked in and I'll show you where your people are staying."

"Thanks." He paused and studied her face. "Do I know you? Could we have met before? You seem familiar."

"No." *Don't let him realize who I am. I don't need to lose the sanctity of my own home. I want to be safe here.* "I've just got one of those faces, a lot of people think they know me." She sure wasn't going to fill him in on her past.

"Okay." He didn't sound convinced.

She breathed a sigh of relief when he glanced around the front entry, used the boot-jack to remove his well-worn cowboy boots. Unless she missed her guess, those puppies were top of the line

Alberta Boot Company boots. It was nice that he shopped Canadian; and he must wear them for more than just show, they'd seen a lot of miles. He placed his boots neatly against the wall and flipped his Stetson onto a wall hook. He didn't even have hat-head? Who didn't get hat-head after wearing a cowboy hat?

"You can leave your boots on, if they're clean. Think of us like a hotel."

He glanced around. "This is your home. I take my boots off at home, I'll take them off here, unless you object."

At a loss for words, she nodded.

"Lead the way, darlin'."

"Darlin'?" She mocked him. "Don't darlin' me. You're a Saskatchewan boy, born and raised outside of Estevan. Don't play up your mock Texas accent on my behalf." She slapped a hand over her mouth. And there it was, her next idiotic move. She'd gone and blurted out the fact that she was a fan and knew his story. Way to alienate your guest! It was as if she'd never taken an on-line university course on running a B&B. Especially the part on respecting a guest's privacy.

"My apologies." He bowed low and tipped an imaginary hat. "Part of the game. I've been doing this so long, I forgot I don't always have to be in star mode." He winked. "Lead on, Steph. The guys will be along shortly."

"So soon? You aren't booked to arrive for hours."

"We got an early start. It won't be a problem, will it?"

"Yes. No. Um—"

"Which is it?" His smirk tickled her funny bone.

"We weren't expecting you for lunch is all. The booking is for dinner, starting tonight. I'll have to see what the chef can work up for you. Expect it to be simple."

"Simple is great. Anything not from a restaurant or room service is a bonus to me. I am several hours early."

"Whew. Follow me."

She pivoted on one stockinged foot and headed down a short

hallway to the office. After confirming his billing information, she printed some forms and slid them across the desk to him. "Read these over and sign beside the red X's, please."

He lifted the pen she placed beside the papers; it disappeared in his large hand. Wow! Nice hands. Down, girl. He'd been here all of five minutes and she was drooling over his hands for the second time. Her hormones did not need this. It had been entirely too long since she had dated, and she didn't want to think about how long it'd been since she'd felt a man's touch. But, dang, the way those hands made a guitar sing, he'd probably work wonders on her hypersensitive skin. Goosebumps rose on her arms just thinking about it.

"Anything else?" He snapped his fingers under her nose.

"What?" Why was he snapping his fingers? How rude was that?

"Where'd you go?" He asked with a wink. "Lost you for a moment there, although I admit, I liked the dreamy look in your eyes. Whoever you're thinking about is one lucky man."

"Um. I don't know about that." She rifled through the paperwork ensuring everything was in order. "I'll just need your credit card."

He extracted a tattered, well-worn, or was it well-loved, wallet from his back pocket and passed over the card. Warm from prolonged contact with his body, it sent tingles down to her toes. Seriously? Tingles? From holding his credit card? She banked a sigh, ran the first batch of charges and struggled to get her lust under control.

"First week went through. I'll need the card again in a week, as per our agreement. We have six rooms in the main house, the rest of your group will stay in the bunkhouse, which has a locking outside door. The inner rooms lock, too. The bunkhouse has a TV and recreation room and its own small kitchen."

"I'm pleased the rooms lock. It'll keep the boys from bickering. I'll be staying in the main house along with my manager, JT. My hand manager, Lola, will be inside, too."

"You have someone to manage your hands?" She must have misheard him. She feigned a wide-eyed, stunned look.

Brett laughed. "Band manager. She's in charge of the setup and takedown guys; roadies. Not my actual hands." He laughed. "Though that is funny. I do have a friend arriving in a few days. He'll take an inside room, as will Mick and Bruce, drummer and bass guitar."

"It's up to you where everyone goes." She showed him two styles of keys. "These ones, with the house-shaped tag are for the bunkhouse. Each set has a room key and a bunkhouse key. They're numbered." She tapped the number on one. "These, with the dog-shaped tags are for the main house. They've got a front door key and a room key. The rooms are labelled by letter."

He studied the keys. "Got it."

"I've put you in Suite A. It's the biggest and has the largest ensuite. Once upon a time it was the master bedroom." She dropped the key into his hand. "I'll keep the second biggest room, B, set aside for your friend. How you divvy up the rest is up to you. Will you be needing all the keys now?"

"How about you give me my key and I'll bring my bags in. Hang onto the rest until we need them."

She returned the keys to the wall cabinet behind the desk. "Supper is at six, everyone eats together. It's a beautiful day, so tonight we'll be barbequing and eating in the picnic area out back. Breakfast is buffet-style from six to nine-thirty."

"And lunch?"

"Like I said, we're not quite ready for you. Give us an hour or so. I've hired an extra cook for your stay. She's agreed to offer a limited menu for lunch between noon and one-thirty. I've set up snack foods in the bunkhouse and lounge areas. If you need more, I'll add it to your bill. Alcohol is allowed, but not provided." She banked an eye-roll. She sounded like a moronic tour guide, not a professional innkeeper. "I lock the main house and the kitchen when I go to bed; but you're free to come and go as you please."

"Yes, ma'am. The band'll be on their best behavior. They're not much for drinking and carousing, contrary to what the tabloids say. And you can rest assured none of them will be inappropriate with you or your staff." He slid his room keys inside his pocket.

"We appreciate that." She gave him her first genuine smile. "You can park your vehicles in the paved lot behind the bunkhouse. Lunch will be in the dining area through those doors. There's another entrance from the outside as well, around back of the house."

When she'd bought her grandparents' ranch from them two years ago, the dining room hadn't existed. There was an enormous eating area off the kitchen but when she'd converted the bunkhouse to extra guest accommodation, she realized the need for more breakfast seating.

She'd renovated the old kitchen and eating area into an enormous professional kitchen and added an addition. The new room butted against the house and was separated by French doors. It had windows on three walls. They started at waist height and rose almost to the ceiling. Currently, it was set up restaurant style, with several small table groupings. They could shift things around if Brett preferred everyone to eat at one large table. It would be tight, but it could be done.

Brett cleared his throat and smiled. "So, Steph, let's go up to my room."

Steph's mouth dropped open. Had she heard him correctly?

"Um, Steph, I just need you to show me the way."

She felt her face flaming. Had he realized where her mind had gone? "Oh, right."

This was going to be the longest three weeks of her life!

CHAPTER 2

"Let me help with that." Brett startled Steph as he lifted the roaster of wrapped, baked potatoes right out of her hands with a grin. "Where do you want this thing?"

"Outside. There's a table next to the barbeque. We'll be eating outside tonight. It's too lovely a day to waste. Thanks for carrying it, but I could have managed." Opening the kitchen door, she waved to the left. "Penny's got the grill fired up. It's about ten minutes to dinner."

She flopped a dishtowel over his shoulder. "Cover them with this please, to keep the heat in."

"Gotcha. I'll be right back to help you carry out the rest of the food."

"You're a guest, not staff." The words bounced off his back as he walked away. It made her uncomfortable when guests helped around the house. A sigh rippled through her and she picked up a tray of mixed salads. Didn't he realize he was a superstar? If the tub hadn't been so heavy and awkward, she'd have insisted on carrying it herself. They'd cooked forty potatoes, enough to feed a small battalion of men. They bought them cheaply from a local grower, and any leftovers would be turned into fried potatoes for breakfast or fed to the pigs. No wasted veggies at the Wild Rose Inn.

He returned way too quickly for her comfort. "What's next?"

"Nothing, you'll be heading outside to enjoy your dinner. You're a guest."

"I like to help out and keep busy. Idle hands are the devil's playground." He winked.

Devil's playground, no doubt. Those hands of his could work some naughty magic with her. Heat rose in her cheeks and she banked the thought for later consideration. No sense revealing her minor case of lust to him.

"And what will you be doing while we eat? You'll be joining us, right?"

"I typically don't eat with the guests. I stay close in case they need something, but I eat in the kitchen. If you shout, I'll hear you. I'll check on everyone throughout the meal, just like a restaurant."

"Why don't you join me, I mean us, for dinner? Please eat with us."

A thrill ran through her. He wanted her company?

"And your cook, too. What's her name again?"

"Penny." Just like that, poof, her thrill evaporated. He didn't want her, he wanted Penny. Bummer. But who wouldn't want to spend time with Penny?

Penelope Flores, Penny was Steph's best friend and she was stunning. She had the fine features of her Caucasian father and the exotic dark beauty of her Mexican mother. Perfectly straight black hair and sparkling black eyes, she was petite and curvy; men couldn't resist her. Why would a superstar like Brett be any different?

"If you want Penny to hang around, you'll have to ask her. I'm not sure of her plans for the evening. Once the cooking is finished, she heads out. The kitchen staff handles the cleanup." Oh lord, she was letting her disappointment show. Not good. She'd better get a grip on herself. Now.

"Actually, we'd like both of you to join us. We spend every waking minute of every day together. Frankly, I'm tired of them. Two pretty faces will be a perfect addition to our crew."

He thought she was attractive? A sparkle of excitement returned. "I'll be happy to join you, although I can't speak for Penny."

"Excellent." He offered his elbow. "If there's nothing left to carry out, may I accompany you to dinner?"

"Indeed, you may." His forearm was muscular and warm under her hand, her fingers twitched with the urge to test his strength and trace the contours of his biceps. She was so far in over her head it wasn't funny, and he'd only been here a couple hours. Three weeks was going to kill her. In all the times she'd thought about him, okay, fantasized about him, she'd never thought him to be humble. She just naturally expected super-star behavior from a superstar. But then, she'd never imagined meeting him, let alone having him stay in her house.

Oh my God! He was sleeping in her house! Her knees buckled. Holy hand grenades, Batman.

"Are you okay?"

She locked her knees and looked up. Their gazes meshed. His pupils dilated, and a slow smile spread across his face. "Everything okay?" Concern edged with something lighter laced his voice.

"Yes." She was half-breathless. "I just stumbled a bit. I'm good. I'm fine." She bit her tongue before the babbling commenced. He unbalanced her equilibrium so easily.

After a quick conversation with Brett and JT, Penny dashed inside to get dishes for herself and for Steph.

Supper was a raucous affair. Nine stagehands and roadies, three band members, Brett and his manager, JT, in addition to Penny and Steph; all sitting at picnic tables in the backyard. It was a party in the making. A lot of laughter and joking. Some of the frivolity was inside jokes beyond Steph's comprehension; yet she didn't feel left out at all. Brett and his crew were entertaining and kept pulling her into their conversation.

Dinner finished, everyone helped move the dishes and leftovers inside to the kitchen. Penny cooked and served, but cleanup fell on other shoulders. One of the roadies disappeared and returned with a couple cases of beer and a cooler of ice, and everyone made their way to the firepit a hundred yards from the house.

Large rocks, almost too heavy to lift, had been rolled into a circle on a concrete platform allowing campfires to be built safely year round. The pit, as it was called, was surrounded by a crushed gravel pad with wooden benches and canvas chairs. With a bit of squishing, there was enough room for everyone.

JT kicked one of the roadies out of the chair beside Penny and took his place. It was only seconds before the pair was deep in conversation and oblivious to everyone else. Brett pulled a canvas chair up beside Steph.

"Mind if I join you?" He settled in without waiting for an answer.

"Help yourself. I won't be out here long. Unfortunately, I have paperwork to do."

"You can't stay? Won't the paperwork wait? It's too lovely an evening to waste indoors." He waved expansively. "Look, the sky's cloud free. In an hour or so, the stars will be brilliant. This could inspire a song. A love song." He caught her gaze and winked.

Dusk hid her flush. "Have you written a lot of songs?"

"Hundreds, maybe thousands. I have stacks of paper everywhere. Someday, I'm going to compile them, maybe organize them. Frankly, a lot of them aren't fit to record. Some are great songs, but not for my voice."

There was sadness under his casual statement. "Are there more like *Laughing Heart*?" She mentioned the song she'd butchered earlier.

"Definitely nothing as good. I think that's my best to date." His humble tone surprised Steph.

"It's my favorite."

"No— I never would have guessed." His laughter rang out; everyone turned to stare.

"Sorry for massacring it."

"Sweetheart, I write music for people to enjoy and you were obviously enjoying it. Watching your *performance* was a pleasure. It certainly isn't something I'm going to forget any time soon."

"Oh, gosh. Can we just drop the subject? I don't ever want to think about it. I'll probably never dance again, either."

"Now, that would be a shame."

She risked another glance at him. His smile was wide, his eyes crinkled at the corners. It was the patented Brett Wyatt grin, with a little extra thrown in. Sincerity? True pleasure? She couldn't be certain, but danged if it didn't reach right into her chest and nudge at her heart. Her breath hitched in her chest. He could seduce her without half trying; she'd best be on her guard during his visit.

"Beer?" He held a bottle toward her.

"No, thanks. I'm more a rye or wine girl. It's chilly tonight." She pulled her bulky sweater closer. "Hot chocolate with a slosh of something with kick would be ideal."

"You're right, cocoa sounds delicious. Marshmallows or whipped cream?"

"I can't have both?"

"A woman after my own heart. The question is, do the marshmallows go over or under the whipped cream?" The look on his face was so serious, you'd think he was discussing the state of world affairs. "I prefer mine under."

She chuckled. "Me, too."

"Brett, get your guitar, play us a song," Penny called out, interrupting their moment.

"Sure, if it's okay with our hostess."

"I'd love to hear you play, please. If you'd like to. I understand if you prefer not to. This is your vacation, you're not here to perform."

"Music is my passion, my life. It's what I do, and who I am. I'd enjoy playing for you." He looked her straight in the eye, as if his words were for her alone. "I'll be back in a flash with my guitar. Do you want a jacket?"

"I'll just throw another log on the fire, I'm good. Thanks."

He nodded and strolled toward the house. Ten minutes later, he hadn't returned.

"Do you suppose he ditched us?" Penny asked. "He's been gone a long time." Before Steph could reply, the back door banged shut. "That must be him."

Brett returned to the fire, guitar case in one hand, two enormous travel mugs in the other. "Your hot chocolate, ma'am. Just the way you requested; marshmallows and whipped cream. I took the liberty of rifling through the kitchen cupboards for supplies. I brought some Baileys with me."

"Thank you!" She reached for the mug he offered. "I don't recognize these mugs."

"Guilty. They're mine. I drink a lot of coffee when I drive. I grabbed them from my rental truck."

"So that's why you were gone so long." She chuckled.

"Did you miss me, darlin'?"

"Don't flatter yourself, superstar." She had missed him, but she'd be darned if she'd reveal that little snippet of information or the fact she'd enjoyed every second she'd spent with him all day. She sipped her cocoa. How had he managed to get it to the perfect drinking temperature?

Brett shuffled his chair, moving it slightly farther away from her, but facing her. He pulled out his guitar and checked the tuning. "Any requests?"

Penny suggested his latest hit. Brett nodded and started strumming. Steph tapped her toes and resisted the urge to get up and dance or sing along. He played quietly and sang along, his voice soft and low. He'd told her he was recovering from his last string of concerts and was resting up for the next.

It didn't matter, even sung low and easy, his voice was beautiful, and this was her one and only chance for a private concert. She was enjoying every minute of it. A few songs later, his voice became hoarse and crackled.

"I guess that's it then. I better stop singing for the night."

Steph watched him for a moment, wondering if there were more to the changes in his voice than just exhaustion; but she chose to leave the question unanswered. She looked around, the band had disappeared into the night. It seemed they'd heard him often enough and they didn't need a private concert.

"That was wonderful," Penny exclaimed. "I'm done. I'm bushed, and I have to get up early."

"I'll walk you to the house." JT stood, and they walked away, hand in hand, leaving Steph alone with Brett.

She leaned back and sighed blissfully. The fire's coals gave off a comforting heat and overhead, the stars danced in and out of wisps of clouds. The moon was barely a sliver in the night sky. A scene romantic enough to make a woman swoon—if she were with the man she loved.

Soft strumming floated through the air, the tune unrecognizable.

"What song are you playing? I thought I knew all your music." Right then, she didn't mind admitting her addiction to his music. "It has a tranquil, lonely sound."

"It's nothing. Just a bit of something that came to me."

"Play more," she whispered. He repeated the notes, fumbled, tried again and dropped the guitar into its case. "Something new?"

"Not yet, but maybe, someday." There was a sad finality to his words which screamed end-of-discussion. She let the subject drop, wondering what nerve she'd touched.

"Thank you for playing. Your music is beautiful."

He nodded his acceptance of her gratitude and her compliment. He tipped his mug up and swallowed the last of his cocoa. "I think I'll turn in. Will the fire be okay?"

"It's almost out, and there's no wind. It'll be fine. I'll check it through the night." She picked up the cooler and dumped the icy water onto the fire. The glow faded and winked out. "There. Perfect."

"Shall we clean up the beer cans?"

Steph glanced around the firepit. "No, I'll bring out the empty boxes and get it tomorrow. There's only a few. Two minutes work. Tops."

He looked her up and down. "You're pretty laid back. I've stayed at a lot of places, tons of bed and breakfasts. You take it pretty easy, but you're professional. You've achieved a nice balance."

"Thanks. I think." She laughed. "I've relaxed a few rules for you guys. I don't typically spend my evenings with guests, or eat with them. Occasionally, I'll join them for breakfast or afternoon tea. I try to judge by the guest. I thought more would like to get to know their host. Some do, some don't. A lot treat The Wild Rose Inn like a hotel and I never see them except at check-in or check-out. I've been doing this for two years now. People like to be left alone, so I try and accommodate where I can. Your group seems to want company and I'll be around when I can."

They walked toward the house. Steph carried the empty cooler, Brett toted his guitar and the coffee mugs. A motion sensor light lit the darkness as they approached the house.

"I appreciate that. It's nice to be treated like a human being, not a star."

"You're a star? Who knew?" She laughed at his shocked expression as they mounted the steps to the porch. "Should I be impressed?" Laughter bubbled over and she giggled aloud. She hadn't felt this good in months, maybe years. "Thank you for the wonderful evening, Mr. Superstar. I enjoyed myself." She propped the cooler open to dry.

"You're quite welcome. Dinner was lovely, I really enjoyed the fire." He stepped closer and paused, inches from her. For three long seconds, she thought he might kiss her. He winked and reached past her to open the door.

"Good night, Brett." She closed and locked the door behind them.

"Good night, Steph." He waggled his fingers, smiled, and headed upstairs.

She watched him until he disappeared around the corner at the top of the stairs, all the while telling herself not to stare at his backside. She left one light burning for guests who wandered downstairs, and entered her office to make her notes on the day's events and guests. She was always careful not to invade on guests' privacy, but at the same time liked to record the memories for the future.

June 15.

Today's guests included country singer Brett Wyatt and his entire entourage. They arrived early. Fortunately, we were almost ready for them, but we did have to throw together an impromptu luncheon. Dinner was barbeque burgers and baked potatoes. We spent the evening by the fire and Brett sang for us. He does have a lovely singing voice, though he tells me he is supposed to be resting his voice between touring sessions. While I don't typically comment on guest appearances, Brett is as handsome as his posters indicate, and has a smile that lights up the room. He's polite and helpful. A girl could easily become distracted by him. But not this girl. I have no room in my life for a superstar who adores the spotlight I so despise. I can't think of anything that would ever put me back in reach of the media. Meeting a famous person has been interesting, although he doesn't act the part of a superstar. He's...humble.

BRETT STARED at the inside of his closed bedroom door. Stephanie Alexander was something else. Gracious, kind, entertaining and unmoved by his stardom. Women like Steph didn't come along every day. He was looking forward to getting to know her better. He laughed aloud thinking of her musical performance when he arrived. It had been totally cringeworthy. But dear lord, the woman could dance. As exhausted as he was when he had arrived, he'd perked right up and paid attention, panting like a dog. If he didn't watch himself, he'd do something stupid like fall for her, and the last thing he needed was a woman sitting around waiting for him. He had no intention of giving up the road and didn't see how a long-term relationship could work if he continued touring.

He shook the thoughts off. What difference did it make? She was just another innkeeper in a long line of places to lay his head. It didn't matter that her pale pink lips were enticingly kissable, and her toned, curvy body cried out for attention.

Nope, it didn't matter one little bit.

CHAPTER 3

"So, this is a working ranch, right?" Brett asked at breakfast the next morning.

"It is, there's another bunkhouse and a foreman's house just over the hill beyond the barns. We had them built when I decided to change the ranch's focus. Why?" She gathered a few mugs and began cleaning up after the meal.

"I saw some guys on horseback and wondered if I could get a tour." He stacked some plates and followed her into the kitchen, his gaze glued to the enticing sway of her hips.

"I can arrange a tour if you'd like. Horseback?"

"Can you take me?" God, he'd love some time alone with her.

"I don't ride."

"What do you mean, you don't ride? You run a ranch." She was adorable when she wrinkled her nose.

"No, I run a bed and breakfast. The ranch is a separate entity altogether. I have a foreman who runs it. Yes, I own it, I oversee it, but I really have nothing to do with it."

"Ah, you're afraid of horses." He was guessing.

"Not afraid, more—wary."

"And why are you wary?" He emphasized the last word.

"I was thrown when I was in my early twenties. I broke my left arm. I like horses. They're beautiful and graceful. I just choose not to ride them anymore."

Oh, she was a little defensive.

"And you bought a bed and breakfast on a ranch, and not someplace else?" Blatant probing for information was likely to get him the slap-down.

"The ranch belonged to my grandparents. They retired and sold it to me. Their only condition was that it remain a functional ranch and that we could continue to have family gatherings here. Like Christmas, Easter, Family Day, and Thanksgiving."

"Is there another way to see the ranch? Could we walk?"

Her laugh sent goosebumps down his spine, straight to his groin. Jesus. He was losing it.

"We could walk the main yard. But the ranch is two miles wide and three miles long. A ten-mile perimeter is a really long walk."

He whistled. "How'd you get such a big spread? What's that in acres?"

"Three thousand eight hundred and forty acres, less some pipeline and road allowances. The land was granted to the family in the late 1800s, as a thank you for fifteen years of service to the government. It's been a working ranch ever since. The original homestead was near the foreman's place. It burned down in a forest fire in 1912. All that's left is the stone foundation and chimney. Someday, I'd like to shore them up and build a cabin using them as a base. I'd like to plant a memorial garden out there, too."

Her smile dimmed. Her face glowed when she talked about the ranch. Her love for the ranch shone in her eyes, echoed by her words; but the memories saddened her.

"A memorial for who?"

"For the family lost in the fire and for a young friend I lost in a tragic accident. Unrelated events; but people worth remembering."

A frown puckered her brow. She shook her head and smiled brightly at him. "Anyway. We could take quads if you wanted a riding tour. Or one of the hands can take you on horseback. Your choice."

"Quads it is then. When do we leave?"

"I'll need an hour at least. I'll meet you back here, after I've taken care of a few things. Bring sunblock if you have it." She hurried to the dining room to finish cleanup.

He watched her go. She was a dynamo. So full of life and energy. She was always cheerful, even if her smile faded on occasion, leaving shadows in her eyes. A couple musical notes rippled through his mind and he hurried upstairs to add them to the few that came last night.

It wasn't a song, yet; but it was a start. Inspiration hadn't visited for months and he was overdue to create something new. Perhaps his muse would find him on this vacation. She was long overdue.

STEPH MADE a few calls and hurried upstairs to change into riding clothes. Quadding required jeans and a long-sleeved shirt at least; if you built up any speed at all, the wind cut right through you. Dressed and ready to go, she skipped downstairs. Brett lounged by the front door, boots on, hat in hand. No man had the right to look so delicious in Wranglers and boots. His checked button-down shirt gave his cowboy look an edge of sophistication.

"Got your sunscreen?"

"Already applied, extra in my pack." He nodded at the tattered leather backpack on the floor at his feet. "Along with a couple water bottles and a first-aid kit."

"Great. I'll just grab a snack from the kitchen and we'll be off."

"I have a snack right here." Penny toted a hamper from the kitchen and placed it at their feet.

After a moment of small talk, Brett picked up the hamper and his bag and gestured toward the door. "Let's go, I'm anxious to see this place." They walked, side by side, down the shale path and over the hill to the barns.

"I called down. They'll have helmets and quads waiting for us."

"Do I need a helmet?"

"That's up to you. I don't wear one myself, but I recommend guests do. If you choose not to, you'll have to sign an additional waiver. The one you signed only covers horseback riding."

"I love when you go all professional innkeeper on me." He chuckled. "So serious and conscientious."

Made uncomfortable by his teasing, she paused and fell a few steps behind him. "It is my job to keep my guests as safe as I possibly can. You take your singing career and your livelihood seriously, why wouldn't I do the same?"

He turned to look at her. "Touché." He touched a finger to the rim of his cowboy hat in salute. "My intention wasn't to make you uncomfortable. You're good at your job and I admire that."

Her insides fluttered and she frowned. "Thank you. So, you'll sign the waiver?"

"Honey, I'll sign anything you want me to if it brings back that pretty smile."

"Flatterer. Let's go. I haven't had a ride in weeks. I'm anxious to feel the wind in my hair. Well, on my face at least." She'd pulled her ponytail through the opening in the ball cap she'd donned earlier. The cap matched the blue in her shirt and the embellishments on her cowboy boots.

"What do you want to see first?" She glanced over at him. He looked perfectly comfortable and competent on the quad. He'd assured her that he'd ridden many times, just not recently. Was there anything he couldn't do?

"I'd like to see the old homestead, if you don't mind? Then maybe some riding in the treed areas. I don't see much forest, living in the city and travelling all the time."

"You've got it. Follow me." It was easier if she led the way, though she wasn't sure she wanted him looking at her butt all the way there. She pushed the thought away. A star like Brett Wyatt had no interest in her backside, even if she adored his.

They rode past the barns and a few paddocks, then made a left and climbed a small hill. She pulled to a stop alongside the old foundation and turned her quad off. She didn't move; she surveyed the land stretched out before her for several moments and finally, looked at the towering chimney and low foundation.

"The foundation and chimney are in surprisingly good shape for their age. They'll both need to be inspected before I determine whether or not to rebuild. One of the hands used to be a structural engineer before the downturn hit and he changed careers. He says they're fixable. Not easily, but without being too costly either. Of course, I'll get an official opinion first."

Brett navigated his way around the remains, pausing now and then to examine them more closely. "I love the flat fieldstone and river rock combination. Who built this? The design is phenomenal, especially the bear and trees. Someone had serious skill to carve solid rock."

"My seven-times great-grandfather built the house; he and his brother designed and built the whole place, even the chimney; as a surprise for their brides. That's why the foundation is so large. The house was two stories, almost a duplex style with a shared kitchen, hearth, fireplace and common room."

"Where'd they live before they built it?"

"Small, separate cabins, long since torn down or reclaimed by nature. They were over there." She waved to the staff bunkhouse. "There used to be a thick bank of pine and spruce trees between here and there. It was selectively logged years ago to finance survival when times were tough. Later, the remaining trees were felled for firewood and to increase our grazing area."

"That's one hell of a history." His admiration glowed in his words. He circumnavigated the foundation again. "I can't imagine building something like this, it's way beyond my skillset."

"Mine too, but I'm glad to live on this land which holds so

much history for our family. We've come close to losing it a time or two. Eight generations have lived, raised children and died here. I'm the last."

She turned away, pretending to take in the scenery while she mustered control over her emotions. Fear of not living up to the family history was a lead weight in her heart. She wasn't likely to meet her future husband holed away on this land; but her past troubles tied her here and her fears prevented her from venturing farther than the nearest town, Okotoks, just half an hour away.

She turned around; Brett stood within arm's reach. Words rushed out of her like water from a broken tap. "The ranch is known to locals as the Alexander place but is officially the Triple-Seven. At one time, my great-grandparents had devoted a large portion of acreage to growing hay. Now, the ranch purchases the hay we need to over-winter the cattle and we graze them on here during the warmer months. It allows us to carry larger stock numbers and not fret about the cost of running and maintaining haying equipment."

"You flip back and forth between me and us. Did you know that?"

"I do?" She tried to recall her words, but nothing concrete came to mind. She'd just spilled words without thinking. "I didn't mean to."

"I think this land means everything to you, like my music means to me." The melancholy in his voice startled her. Before she could question it, he hopped on his quad. "Let's go exploring. I want to see more." He fired up his machine; the noise made it difficult to talk without shouting.

She remounted and they drove down the other side of the hill. She toured him through several areas, stopping often to open and close gates, ensuring the cattle stayed where they were meant to be. Pastures were grazed in succession, each one left to regenerate before the cattle returned.

Eventually, they paused beside a small stream and spread out a blanket for a picnic.

"For someone who doesn't ranch, you sure know a lot about it." Brett winked.

"I should. I was raised here. I lived here until I graduated high school at seventeen. I moved to Calgary and received an education at the U of C. I have my degree in elementary education."

"And you don't teach?"

"I did for a while. But then my grandparents wanted to retire and two years ago, I came home."

"What about your folks?"

She opened the basket and started pulling out food. "Dad hated ranching. He sold farm equipment until he retired. Now, he and Mom are jet-setting around the world, travelling and having a blast. They live off savings and the money Mom inherited from her folks."

"No siblings?"

"A brother, Thomas, and a sister, Francine. They hate the ranch. Sure, they come home every holiday, but they can't wait to be gone again. That's why I bought the place." She passed him a soda. "Look, enough about me. Let's talk about something else."

Good gravy! She'd nearly bared her soul to him. If she'd kept talking, he'd learn about the court settlement she'd received after being wrongfully charged in the death of a school boy under her watch. That was a story she had no intention of sharing with him, or anyone else. "Tell me about the famous Brett Wyatt."

She finished setting out their luncheon. An enormous meal by her standards, but for a fully grown and rather large man, probably just adequate. "Here we go. Ham and cheese sandwiches on fresh, homemade rolls. Cheese and crackers, grapes and strawberries and a thermos of coffee. And a couple sodas. Chocolate cake for dessert."

"Woman, you tempt me. I eat way too many meals in restaurants, choking down room service meals. Don't even ask me about my own cooking." He shuddered, and she laughed. "If you keep feeding me like this, I'll gain fifty pounds in three weeks. My stage career will die when I lose my looks and I'll be forced to live off your goodwill forever."

"Oh, you poor baby." She reached over and patted his cheek. She lingered for half a second, her palm pressed against his smooth cheek. Gracious, he was soft and warm under her hand. She dropped her hand and sucked in a breath. Sweet heaven, he even smelled delicious.

She grabbed a plastic container and yanked it open. Crackers exploded everywhere. They covered the blanket, the grass. One landed on Brett's hat. She plucked it off, ignoring his laughter as she picked up the mess.

"Nicely done. Do you always throw your food around?"

"Rarely." She fought to keep a straight face but failed. "So, what about you?"

"I'm just a poor country boy with a guitar."

"Right. Sell me another one."

"A rich country boy with a guitar?" He quirked one eyebrow before filling his plate.

"Family?" She carefully placed a few strawberries and some cheese on her plate, ignoring the sandwiches altogether.

"Two brothers, highly successful. A family doctor and a lawyer. They made my family proud." His brow wrinkled.

"And you didn't?" Who wouldn't be proud of a country music superstar? She followed his career, he had a good reputation, didn't party much and there were few, if any, rumors of women or drugs.

"They didn't care for my music when I had my first garage band in grade seven. It took me over a year to save up enough money for my first battered guitar. Sure, they let me play, but when I started touring with a small band right out of high school, they weren't impressed. It took me ten years to become an 'overnight success' as the media calls me. We played the worst shit-hole bars for years. All for the love of music. I pumped gas between gigs."

"Wow, I had no idea. The press talks about your small town, country roots, and your sudden fame. They left the rest out."

"Part of the game, darlin'. My publicist and I came up with a history. All true, just carefully edited to keep my family out of it. They don't need to be bothered by my fame."

She jumped to her feet. "Bothered by your fame?" She paused, hands on hips and frowned. "Buttered biscuits. That's crazy. You've earned every minute of your fame. You don't act like a superstar at all. They should be danged proud of you."

∽

Brett stared up at the dynamo in front of him. She was beautiful in her angry defense of him. Her wrinkled brows, her frown and those flashing brown eyes. Such anger, all in his defense. He couldn't recall anyone, ever, standing up for him like she had. She'd knock his family on their judgmental asses. Something stirred in his heart. He swallowed hard. The discomfort in his guts wasn't because her fire was affecting him, he must be eating too fast. He'd better slow down. But, holy moly, she was stunning with her cheeks flushed, pacing back and forth.

"Come, sit." He patted the blanket. "I'm a big boy. I learned long ago that I don't need my family's approval to survive." Why did his long acceptance of their behavior suddenly feel like a copout, a justification? They were who they were and he loved them; he wished they understood why music was so important to him.

"Isn't family important to you?" She dropped down to the blanket and poured herself a coffee. He shook his head when she held the pot up to him.

"I love my family, but I can't change who they are. They don't understand my career, I get that. I can't fathom how Steve can stomach criminal law. Not understanding doesn't mean not loving."

He flopped onto his back and watched the clouds skitter past in the pristine blue sky.

"It's like this. They're my family. But I have another family. My band, my road crew, my manager, my friends. Even my fans. Do you know what it's like to have someone write you and tell you how you changed their life? It's beyond incredible to know you've helped someone through a rough time." Attempting to move away from the awkward conversation, he pointed to a cloud. "Look, there's a guitar."

"You're looking at it wrong. It's a pot-bellied pig."

Her laugh trickled down his body, lodging in his groin. He raised one leg, blocking her view of his unexpected, uncontrollable reaction to her. "Typical rancher response. That one," he pointed again, "is a dragon."

"It's Pegasus."

"Are you trying to cause a fight?" He rolled his head to look at her.

"Are you avoiding talking about your family?" she countered.

The woman was as dogged as a pit bull; she wasn't going to let this go.

"Yes." He was silent for a few moments, thoughts pinging through his head like mixed-up lyrics to half-forgotten songs colliding discordantly. "My music is my life. I love composing and singing. And the rush I get when I'm on stage—there's nothing comparable. Sure, there are days when the exhaustion is overwhelming and the fans annoying. But that's a minor inconvenience compared to the bliss of playing and singing." He found himself wondering if his voice echoed his enthusiasm. *Did his passion come through? Could a virtual stranger realize how important this was to him?*

"Couldn't you play and sing without touring? I'm sure you can write music anywhere, right?" The question popped into her mind and out of her mouth before she realized it was coming. "I can't imagine a lonelier life than travelling all the time. What about love, kids, marriage? Doesn't that matter to you?"

Yikes! What was she doing asking such personal questions? She'd lost her mind.

"I know, it's none of my business. Forget I asked."

"It's okay. We're just chatting. I trust you won't share our conversations with anyone, particularly reporters?"

"On my honor. I'd never divulge guests' conversations or secrets. Anything you say to me is confidential. I expect the same of my staff. Although in reality, I cannot guarantee their silence, most of them are temps hired for your stay. So, tread carefully." Unease niggled at her conscience. She had no real control over her staff, what if one of them spoke out of turn? She wouldn't have hired them if she didn't think they were trustworthy, but there was always an element of doubt. Her regular chambermaid and Penny wouldn't talk out of turn. Hopefully, the rest would take her policy on confidentiality to heart.

"I'm not opposed to a long-term relationship; but I'm not prepared to give up touring. It's a lifestyle I love. The travel is exhausting but performing live is the highlight of my life. I can't fathom another way to live; this is all I've known since leaving home. I don't see how the two lifestyles could be compatible; unless my partner chose to travel with me and it's unfair to ask anyone to give up their life to accommodate mine."

"Don't you long for a home?" Travelling continually and living in the spotlight was her worst nightmare. Being a Stampede princess had been great. It had been tiring, but she'd loved every minute of it. Her second brush with fame had nearly ruined her. There was no way she wanted to go there again. Although, admittedly, his fame was positive. Hers? Not so much.

"I have a home. In Toronto. I own a two-level penthouse suite on the thirtieth floor. Ten thousand square feet of luxury living with an amazing view of Lake Ontario. It's where I go to relax between tours."

"Why aren't you there now?"

"The crew wanted to spend time together, off duty. Some of them will be in and out, visiting family and friends. All of them are single, so a few weeks with easy access to the mountains was a perfect solution. A friend recommended your place, so here we are. You and I enjoying a picnic in the country."

Could a person really be that casual and unconnected to their living space? And the way he talked about it, like it was a possession not a home. Everyone knew he was rich, but his comments seemed... not greedy, exactly, or materialistic. Was he all about the money?

"I don't think I could live the touring lifestyle. I like my home, and my privacy."

"My music is more important than anything to me at this point in my life. Things could change, but I don't think I'll ever tire of the spotlight or the music."

She didn't say anything for a moment, considering his words. On the surface, this was a civil conversation, deeper down it seemed more a philosophical disagreement. It shouldn't matter, he was a stranger, albeit a very attractive one, passing through her life. No different than any other guest. She wanted more for him. A tiny voice, deep inside her heart, whispered she wanted more *from* him. She lay on the blanket beside him, searching the clouds for answers to unformed questions.

"Put your head on my shoulder, you'll be more comfortable."

Yeah, right. Like she'd do that. Was he inviting her for more than just comfort? No way. A fling wasn't in the cards for her. She had too much baggage for a regular relationship. She pondered the thought. Her belly cramped. Maybe a fling was just what she needed; a bit of intimacy, without the ties and long-term connection. It was two years since her ex had dumped her in the wake of the disastrous lawsuit and publicity after the accident.

She sat up and avoided the decision. "I think I'll have a bit more lunch."

"Avoiding me?"

Her breath caught in her throat. Did he want more? Why would a superstar want her?

"No. I'm just hungry."

"Can we at least be honest with each other? I like you, Stephanie Alexander, and I'd like to get to know you better."

She didn't look at him, but his muscular forearms and flat stomach were burned into her mind as if she'd stared at him for hours. Her fingers twitched. She wanted to lean on him, to touch him. She picked at the crackers and cheese.

"I'll start."

"You'll start what?" She peeked up to look at him. He was deadly serious, no hint of frivolity on his face.

"I'll start the getting to know each other."

She nodded.

"You asked me last night if I was playing a new song. I was, sort of. I haven't written a new song since my last album released. Those few notes were the first bit of inspiration I've had in two years. My inspiration is dead. Gone. I'm not sure it'll come back. That's why travelling, touring, is so important. It's all I have left." His voice cracked on the last words.

She opened her mouth to respond, snapped it shut and tried again. Nothing. She swallowed hard. Finally, she found her voice. "It'll come. I believe in you. You've got too much talent for it to just dry up and wither away. Sometimes a change of scenery can break something free. Perhaps, The Wild Rose Inn and the Triple-Seven Ranch will be the catalyst for your muse to return."

"I damn well hope so." He paused. "Sorry for swearing. I hope you're right. Perhaps you'll be just what I need to create again. Maybe being with you will inspire me. You inspired those few notes, perhaps, with time, you'll give me more."

Holy sinners! If that wasn't enough pressure to send a girl fleeing into the forest, she didn't know what was.

"I'm not sure what you want. I've only known you twenty-four hours. You're passing through. You don't want what I want." Dang, she was putting the cart ahead of the horse. He wasn't offering anything except a shoulder to lean on.

"True, but you're a very attractive woman, and I'm a red-blooded male. I'm not suggesting anything. I just want to get to know you better. Lying here, talking seemed a good place to start. You might as well be comfortable."

Okay, maybe he was offering more. She felt like a dithering idiot. It'd been an eternity since she was in a social situation, guests not included; she'd lost any gift she'd possessed for reading people. She pulled her knees to her chest and wrapped her arms around them. Resting her cheek on one knee, she stared into the distance, looking away from the temptation lying beside her.

"Want to do a fence run?" she blurted.

"A what?"

"A fence run. There's a trail around the perimeter of the ranch. We ride quads all the way round and make note of any fencing issues. It's fast, it's fun. You'll see some great scenery. Consider it a day at the ranch, a working holiday." *Let him say yes. Let him say yes.* The words were a litany running through her head. The seconds it took him to decide felt like an eternity. Time might fly when you're having fun; but is was slower than molasses in January when you were trying to change the subject to avoid conversation.

He shifted beside her. She straightened to look at him.

"Did I say something wrong?" His ubiquitous smile was missing, his eyes flat without sparkle. "I didn't mean to push or be offensive."

"No. It's good. I just thought you might want to do something more interesting than sitting here." Oh, sweet heaven, she was going to burn in Hell for lying.

"Okay then. Let's ride." He jumped to his feet and shoved some containers into the picnic basket. She helped him pack everything up.

With the basket secured, she reached for the key to her quad.

"I don't know what I said, but I apologize. You're an attractive woman and you don't seem moved by my fame. It's nice. I like it. I like you and I didn't mean to make you uncomfortable."

"Thanks." She nodded, firing up her machine, then before he mounted his, she was riding away. Ugg. She was such a moron. Jumping from one conclusion to the next with no idea what reality was. Beside him, she felt unstable, like she was standing on a cliff with the edge crumbling beneath her boots and nothing to grab to check her fall. Did he have to be so nice? Three weeks with Brett Wyatt as her guest was going to test her sanity to the limits. Could she get through without saying anything else stupid, or more importantly, could she keep from kissing him? Only time would tell. As for inspiring him? Pure flattery on his part. He had an endgame and she'd figure out what it was.

CHAPTER 4

Breakfast had come and gone and the band roadies had dispersed to entertain themselves. Brett was upstairs in his room, practicing guitar. She'd listened at the door for a moment, until shame for eavesdropping drove her away. He was playing, but not singing. He'd mentioned resting his voice again last night.

Penny was prepping salad for supper while Steph cleaned and sterilized the stainless-steel counters and wiped down the appliances. All part and parcel of the usual routine. It was a chance to work and chat together.

"Well, if you aren't just a sight for sore eyes." A deep masculine voice rumbled through the kitchen, startling Steph.

That voice! She knew that voice! She whirled round to find Tucker Marcus standing in the doorway. He looked incredible. His dark brown eyes shone with happiness, and a wide smile creased his ebony face. Despite the frown lines at the corner of his eyes, he looked better than any time in the past two years. Things must be turning around.

"Tucker!" She dropped her dishcloth and threw her arms

around his waist and grinned up at him. Penny let out a small delighted squeal.

"Hey, girl. How's things? You getting by okay?" He returned Steph's hug with double enthusiasm. "I haven't seen you since you left Toronto." A shadow passed across his face, but the smile returned almost as bright as before.

"Yeah, let's not talk about the past. Okay? How are you? What are you doing here? How's life and work?"

"Whoa there, girlie." He kissed the top of her head. "Take a breath. You always did chatter too much when you were excited. I remember when you finally managed to teach Elijah to tie his shoes. You rambled on about it for fifteen minutes before Anita and I got a word in edgewise. My boy was almost as proud as you were. You should go back to teaching. What happened wasn't your fault, nobody blames you."

She stepped away and wrapped her arms around her middle. So much for the thrill of greeting an old friend. Two years ago, Elijah Marcus, Tucker's son, had been in her grade one class. Now, he was dead, and it was her fault. "Anita blames me."

"Anita's a selfish cow. Her beauty doesn't go beyond the pretty façade. She doesn't care about anyone except Anita. Elijah was just an extension of herself. She paraded him around like he was a toy and stuffed him away when she had better things to do." Disdain dripped from his words. "We're divorced and it's the best thing that ever happened to me."

"Oh, Tucker. How horrible. I didn't know. All the times we talked—you never told me." She patted his arm and hugged him again. His shoulders were broad enough she could barely get her arms around them. "You're doing okay, then?"

He laughed deeply, his bald head thrown back in pleasure. "Girl, you care too much for everyone else. It's why I always loved you, from the moment I first saw you teaching Elijah how to read. Anita and I kept the divorce a secret for a long time. We tried counselling, but our relationship was weak before Elijah passed. After that, there was no going back."

"So, it's my fault." The guilt she'd never managed to escape from or forget stabbed her in the guts like a physical blow. Her mouth tightened, and her smile turned downward. In two minutes she'd gone from elation at seeing an old friend to borderline depression. She closed her eyes and breathed deeply. In for three, out for three. She called up a happy moment with Elijah and reached for the joy.

Memories of Tucker's son were bittersweet. He'd been one of her favorite students and despite his passing, was still a source of joy for her. He hadn't always been a favorite, but her therapist had taught her to embrace the good memories and then use them to enhance the present.

"It's not your fault. It never was. The press, the school board, the pool, they were just casting blame where none lay. My son's death was a tragic accident and it isn't your fault, it never was."

"Come on, Tucker, you know that's not true. I've accepted my culpability in the incident. I should have been more vigilant."

"We're not having this argument again. When the fire at the pool broke out, you rushed in, fully clothed, and saved six kids while the lifeguards panicked."

"I should have gone back in for Elijah. I didn't know he was still in the water." Tears rolled down her face and a sob burst from her throat. She swallowed hard. "Tucker, I'm so sorry."

He picked her up and set her on the counter. He cupped her face in his enormous black hands and stared into her eyes. "Listen to me, Stephanie Alexander. What happened is not your fault. It never was. Fault lies with the pool's shitty maintenance. The media circus that followed was unacceptable and to this day, I know that if I get my hands on one of the reporters who hounded you with blame, I swear to God, I'll end them."

He shook her gently and wiped away her tears with his thumb before he spoke again. "I'm good. Anita's good. She acts like it never happened, she's in denial. And you, Penny tells me you're doing better every day. Although, you still won't venture beyond Okotoks."

"There aren't many reporters in Okotoks. I still avoid the city. I tried Christmas shopping there last year. It just figures I'd end up at Southcentre Mall on the same day as a celebrity. I thought I'd be safe this far from Toronto. One of the reporters recognized me. It was the same media gong-show all over again. I've had my five minutes of infamy. I don't need more."

The nightmare after Elijah's death had nearly ruined her. She wasn't a weak person, or suicidal, by any stretch, but there'd been times when she wondered if she wouldn't be better off dead. Thank God, her family had talked her into seeing a therapist. Two years after he died, she still had a video conference with her shrink once a week. At least it wasn't every day now, and she'd been weaned off her anti-depressants. Small victories.

"I'll be okay as long as I stay out of the city and the big crowds."

"You're one hell of a woman. So, where's the superstar?"

"What superstar?" She feigned ignorance. Sometimes, he talked with Penny when he called; had she told him about Brett Wyatt being here? If she had, she'd wring Penny's neck like the chicken for Sunday dinner. It was bad enough Penny told Tucker all her secrets, she had from the first time he called when Steph wasn't in the house. But divulging information on a guest was a firing offence, best friend or not.

"I sent him here." Tucker laughed. "I'm his lawyer and his friend. The man's making me rich." He laughed loudly and slapped one hand on his thigh.

Tucker Marcus had always been bigger than life. Happy go lucky, he was a joy to be around. They'd become friends in the eight months Elijah had been in her class. That friendship was strained for a while after his death, the stress and memories had been too much. But, he'd stood beside Steph in support through the whole disaster and as time passed, they'd started communicating again. It was because of Tucker's legal skills and connections that the papers and the pool had been forced to pay Steph out for false accusations and slander. It hadn't even gone to trial. She'd used the money to buy and upgrade the ranch. She wasn't sitting pretty, but she wasn't destitute either.

Initially, there'd been guilt, so much guilt over taking the money. But, she'd bought herself a future and had plans to use the rest of the money to help kids. She just wasn't sure how yet. She had an idea rolling around in the back of her mind, it just wasn't fully formed. Maybe if she built more guest quarters, especially for kids…

No sense trying to force the idea forward. It would come when it was ready. When it popped up, she'd craft a business plan and take the remains of her settlement out of the high interest account it was in and get moving.

She hopped off the counter and leaned against it. "You sent Brett here?"

"He did."

She turned. Brett stood in the kitchen doorway. A deep frown marred his face.

"What can I do for you, Brett?"

"You can explain the conversation I just overheard. I knew I recognized you when I checked in. Your face was all over the papers when Elijah died." His voice sliced through the room like a sword and jabbed into her guts. His frown deepened, his fists bunched and he stomped into the kitchen.

"I don't believe I'm required to fill customers in on my personal life." She kept her tone light and professional, despite the trepidation clawing at her heart. Not again. She didn't want to have to relive this again. She couldn't survive another round of heartache.

"You knew who she was and still sent me here?" Brett turned on Tucker.

"Her past is in the past. It has nothing to do with the present or with you, my friend." Tucker leaned on the counter beside Steph and slung his arm casually over her shoulder.

"I'm just going to run to the storeroom and find more coffee filters." Penny squished past Brett and disappeared. Steph had forgotten her friend was in the room.

"Elijah was my godson. You should have told me."

Steph stared him down. Between his glare and her guilt, it was all she could do not to cut and run and leave Tucker to deal with his friend. "I didn't realize you two knew each other." *Great, now she was making inane comments instead of rational conversation.*

"We've been friends for years. Don't worry about Brett. He's all bark and no bite. He loved Elijah. We all did. I should have warned him."

~

"Yeah, you should have. I'd have stayed elsewhere. I can't believe you're friends with her.

God, how could Tucker stand to be that close to her? She was responsible for Elijah's death. He spared her another glance. Tears trickled down her cheeks, her skin had lost its color. She looked awful.

Damn.

"I tried to save all the kids," she whispered, her voice shaking. "I saved six others. If I'd known Elijah was still in the water, I'd have gone in again. I had second degree burns on a third of my body, but I'd take triple that to bring him back. I'd gladly trade my life for his."

She wrapped her arms around herself and stared at the floor. She seemed to shrink, right in front of his stare.

"You're a fucking asshole." Tucker reached out and punched Brett in the shoulder. It hurt like a bitch and he had to clench his fists to keep from retaliating.

"What happened wasn't Steph's fault. I blamed her, blamed her for a few days. Then the truth came out and I realized the fault lay elsewhere. Man up. Stop being a dick. Would I have sent you here if I thought she was guilty? Dip-shit."

Something heavy and uncomfortable squeezed at Brett's chest. Shit. He was being an ass. It wasn't like him to be irrational. But, dammit, he was attracted to her. She was beautiful and didn't care about his fame. It was disappointing to know she'd been Elijah's teacher.

"I'm happy to refund the cost of your stay if you wish to leave." She didn't look up. A tear fell and splashed soundlessly on the floor in front of her.

Double-damn.

"Are you nuts?" Tucker demanded and bumped her with his hip. "If the jerk wants to leave, he can; but you're not giving him a damn refund."

"I'm staying."

This time she did look up. Her eyes were red, her face streaked with tears. Anger flushed her cheeks. His heart stuttered. Hellfire. He'd messed up good.

"You operate on the mistaken assumption that I intend to allow you to stay. I won't be abused in my own home. Take your band and your guitar and cram them where the sun don't shine. Be gone before dinner."

Tucker gasped.

Brett stared at the two of them, banded together, arm in arm, united against him. Tucker was supposed to be his best friend. And Steph… dear God, he was attracted to her, more than he wanted to admit. For a while, he thought she might be attracted to him, too. He'd killed that. How the hell did he fix this?

He wasn't one to act or speak impulsively. After years of life in the public eye, he knew to keep his mouth shut. He'd lashed out in pain. Elijah was like a son to him; his death had been a blow and at least part of the reason he'd stopped writing lyrics. The last song he'd composed had been a light-hearted ditty devoted to Elijah. Before he died.

"I don't suppose we can talk about this?"

"I don't see why we should. Clearly you consider me guilty without knowing all the facts. Far be it for me to disagree with a superstar. You can leave anytime."

Her words were brave and defiant, but he heard the tremor in her voice. Her arms tightened around her waist until he thought she'd squeeze herself in half. Damn. Hadn't he faced enough rumor and innuendo in the tabloids to teach him not to act on half information. Hell, he didn't even have half information. He was such a moron.

He paced over to the small staff table and dropped into a chair and raked his fingers through his hair. "I'm sorry. I overreacted. Let's start this conversation again. Please." Tucker and Steph stared at him without answering. For half a second, he debated turning on his country-singer charm. He discarded the notion. These people were his friends, not fans or the media. They deserved better.

"Elijah's death hit me hard. When I think about it, I still reel. He was my godson and I rarely ever saw him. I should have come home more often. I shouldn't have let my manager book me so heavily. I lost so much time with him; and now, I can't get it back." He stopped talking and formulated his thoughts. "Tucker told me Elijah drowned on a school outing. That's all I know. I couldn't bear to watch the news or read the papers. I chose to bury my head in the sand. What else do I need to know?"

He looked between Tucker and Steph, waiting for one of them to speak. They looked at each other. Tucker nodded and Steph turned toward Brett. Her eyes still shone with tears, but her face had a bit more color.

"We went on a pool outing. Not lessons, just a fun swim. We had one parent chaperone for every five kids. Some men, some women. The pool had extra lifeguards on because grade one children have such differing skill levels and need extra supervision.

There were parents in the water, and some watching from the pool deck." Her voice shuddered, and she swallowed hard.

"I was on deck. Everything was great. The kids were having a blast. The parents were attentive. There was a loud rumbling sound and a huge crack. Something gave way. They're still not sure what happened, something exploded. Sparks flew everywhere and the entire deck caught fire." She shuddered. "I never would have thought you could catch a swimming pool on fire. Everything but the water was burning."

She drew in a shuddering breath. "Kids started screaming. Parents were running everywhere. I froze. I panicked."

Tears streamed down her face and Brett clenched his fists to keep from going to her. He needed to hear this, without interruption.

"One of the lifeguards dove in and started pulling kids from the water. The other lifeguards panicked. Parents hustled kids into the change rooms. I saw one child go under the water and not come up. I raced into the water and pulled him and a girl to the deck. I went in four times. The screaming was insane. It echoes in my nightmares." She grabbed a paper towel and blew her nose into it and wiped the tears away.

"I didn't know. I swear to God, I didn't know Elijah was still in the water. With all the flames and smoke, and a beam across the water, I didn't see him. I'd have gone back for him, despite my burns. I'd have given my life to save him. I didn't know." She broke down into shuddering sobs and turned to Tucker for comfort.

He wrapped his arms around her and patted her back, tears ran down his face and into her hair. Their bodies shook with silent sobs, their grief palpable. Brett realized he was crying, too. God, what she must have gone through.

"I'm sorry. I'm so sorry. For being an ass, for what you went through." He stood and paced the kitchen. "I had no idea. No freaking idea. I can't even imagine." Thoughts ping-ponged around his brain. She had to have survivor guilt. The loss. The pain. The senseless tragedy. He couldn't form another sentence; hell, he could barely form a coherent thought.

Tucker spoke, "I learned yesterday that the investigation proved the pool's maintenance was sub-standard. They've been charged and a trial is pending. But the pool, the city, and the papers: every single media outlet who blamed Steph has paid her a settlement for false accusations. She could have died saving those kids. And, don't be thinking she profited from it. She deserved every penny and more for her heroic deeds. She loved Elijah as much as you and I did."

God, he wanted to puke. How had she survived the aftermath, the press? No wonder she seemed so against being in the spotlight. He choked down the lump in his throat.

"Oh, my God. I'm so sorry you went through such hell. I can't apologize enough for being an asshole." She nodded without moving her head from Tucker's chest. "I'll pack my things and leave. Please let the band stay."

∼

Steph was tempted to let him go. He'd acted like a jerk. Now, she heard remorse in his voice, and grief. She didn't want to kick him out, nor did she want him to stay. Indecision wracked her.

"What do you say, Steph? Can he stay? I took my vacation to see the two of you. To spend time with my friends. He's a jerk and deserves to be kicked out for being an ass; but deep down inside, somewhere beneath his superstar idiocy, he's still the same kid I once played band with. He's got a good heart, it's just not as big as his ego."

She puffed out a ragged breath. She was cornered between them. She really didn't have a choice, even if it meant she'd need extra therapy sessions once he left. "Fine. He can stay. Only because you asked me. If it was just him, I'd as soon run over him with a quad."

"Ouch. I deserved that. I'll try and stay out of your hair. Again, I apologize for being rude."

"And a jerk, and inconsiderate, and a wiener and an ass," Tucker added in a tone halfway between a laugh and chastisement.

"Guilty on all charges."

Brett sounded contrite. His eyes were heavy with shame. She looked deep inside her heart. Could she find a way to forgive him? He'd only responded the same way as the media and everyone else had; with angry, demeaning comments. Nonetheless, nerves raw and on edge, she was disinclined to forgive him. Her shrink's voice was echoing in her head, spouting lines about forgiveness and a better life.

"I'll try not to be too uncomfortable around you. I will. Please carry on like any other guest. There won't be anymore private tours, though. Stay. Spend time with Tucker." She tried, and failed, to make the words gracious and understanding. He'd opened old wounds and inflicted new ones. It would take her time to heal.

"Don't be a dick, or I'll beat the crap out of you." Tucker teased. "You'll look like an idiot on stage with your face messed up."

"Tucker!" Steph admonished. "You'll do no such thing. I'm not saying he doesn't deserve it, but violence doesn't solve anything."

"I can't apologize enough and I swear I'll be on my best behavior. I'll leave you two to catch up. Tucker, I'll see you later." His smile was awkward and obviously forced. He nodded and left her alone with Tucker.

"Wow." She sighed. "That sucked." She faked a laugh.

Tucker cussed.

CHAPTER 5

Brett avoided Steph like the plague over the next few days. Every time she caught his eye, he looked away. If she tried to approach him, he left the room. It was getting ridiculous. She couldn't decide if he was embarrassed over how he'd behaved, was being careful not to annoy her, or if he still blamed her for Elijah's death. She wanted to talk to him about it, to make him feel more comfortable, but he didn't give her an opportunity.

The tension between them was awkward and unnecessary as far as she was concerned. After several failed attempts to talk to him, she approached the lion in his den. Outside his closed door, she listened to him softly strumming his guitar. When he reached the end of the song, she knocked lightly.

"Come in."

She opened the door and peeked her head inside. "I'd like to talk to you for a moment."

He looked down and picked at the strings of his guitar, plucking a discordant melody. "About?"

He was going to make this difficult for her; but she'd persist because the stiffness between them was filtering down to his band. Even Tucker had mentioned it.

"Listen, there's tension between us, and I'd like to know what I can do to lighten it. When you arrived, we had a comfortable relationship. Knowing my past has made you wary of me; I understand that. But, the past is done. I can't go back and change it, though I would if I could."

She paused, waiting for him to speak. After two minutes of silence with only the sound of his guitar between them, she mustered her courage and went on, before the discomfort crushed her. Without asking, she strolled into the room and perched on the edge of the navy wing chair under the window. She stared outside at the lawn and garden before speaking.

"Elijah was my student. My favorite, actually. It was my tenth anniversary year with the school board. They'd hired me right out of university. Part time at first, but I subbed for maternity leave almost immediately as the woman never returned to teaching. I'm not sure how I scored the job. I was shocked someone with more union seniority didn't snap it up. Good school, great principal and a nice neighborhood. Not rich, not poor. A comfortable middle class."

Memories swirled around her. The kids. The laughter. The tears. Fights. Cliques. The amazing sense of accomplishment when a small face brightened with sudden understanding.

"I can't describe what it was like. The highs, or the lows. I made so many friendships, with teachers, parents and students. Last week, I had a visit from one of my very first students. He's headed off to university in the fall. Lacrosse scholarship. We've communicated off and on since he was in my class. He came to thank me for persisting and helping him learn to read. We spent hours after school all year. Phonics was the ticket, but the progress had been slow. Once he got it, he couldn't stop reading. He graduated a year early."

"That must have been satisfying."

"It was, but he wasn't the only one. Every year, there was a new problem or an old one needing a new solution. Elijah was brilliant, but socially awkward. Terrified of girls, except me. And physically —well, you know how he was. Uncoordinated and tripping over his feet. With Tucker's height and Anita's long legs, he was destined to be tall and thin. He shot up so fast."

"He grew so much that year. I saw him on Easter break. He tripped over everything. But he was so proud, he'd learned to tie his shoes. His 'favorite' teacher taught him." He stopped strumming and looked up. "It must have been you."

"We practiced every day."

"The rabbit thing." He laughed sadly. "I remember it."

Pride rushed over her. She'd taught him that! And, he'd shared it with Brett. More memories flooded in. Elijah babbling on about his best friend, Brett, who came to dinner when he could. But, not often, cause he *workded* out of town.

"You were going to teach him to play." The revelation was startling. "He told me you got him a guitar for his birthday. A real one, not a toy. You gave him lessons on Skype."

"He loved those lessons." Brett's frown lightened. It wasn't a smile yet, but it was close.

"He brought it to school for show and tell. He played for the entire class. He wasn't shy at all. He told us he was going to be just like his friend when he grew up. He'd have a band and sing songs to make people smile. Gosh, he was so proud of you."

Their gazes met, and they shared a soft smile.

"I wish I'd been there to see him." His arms crossed and he rubbed his shoulders, his expression wistful.

"Wait." She jumped up. "I've got it on DVD. I recorded it on my phone." She grabbed his hand and tugged. "Come downstairs, to the entertainment room. I'll show you. You'll love it."

Stepping back, she waited for him to slide his guitar into the case before she hurried downstairs to find the disc.

"Sit there, on the couch. Best seat in the house." She waved toward the seat as she slid the disc in the player and adjusted the sound. Remote in hand, she dropped beside him on the couch, close, but not quite touching. She fast-forwarded the video through some other children's presentations and grabbed his hand. "This is it. Right now. I've watched it a hundred times." Brett squeezed her hand between his. She glanced at him, his eyes were scrunched tightly shut.

On the video, she said. *"Elijah, you're up next."*

Brett's eyes popped open.

Shuffling sounds followed and Elijah came forward on the screen, lugging his guitar case with him.

"I'm Elijah Marcus. My best friend, Brett, gave me this guitar for my birthday. He's teaching me to play." He opened the case and showed the guitar off before slipping the strap over his head. He strummed awkwardly and played Three Blind Mice and ABCs.

"I taught him that," Brett whispered, his voice hoarse with emotion and pride.

"I'm learning another one, but I'm not too good yet. It's a surprise for Brett. Nobody's heard it, except now you guys. I'll play it for him when he comes to visit me." He strummed a bit and started singing Laughing Heart, Brett's latest hit. The playing was awkward and the singing off-key and enthusiastic, but the pride in his eyes was beautiful. He finished and bent to place the guitar in the case, the class erupted in applause. When asked, he let the other children hold the guitar and showed them how to strum.

"He was so proud to be your friend, and to have you teach him. He talked about it all the time. I had no idea Brett was you, even though he played your song. I should have put two and two together." Steph turned off the video and looked at Brett. Tears rolled unchecked down his cheeks and his body shook with silent sobs, but the smile on his face was ten miles wide.

"Thank you. Oh God, Steph, thank you. I can't repay you enough for this." He pulled her hand to his mouth and kissed it.

"I'll make you a copy."

"Me too." She whirled around at the sound of Tucker's strained voice. "That's my boy. I've never seen this video." His voice was puzzled, but accusation free. Like Brett, Tucker was teary eyed and smiling.

"Two copies it is. I'm sorry I never showed you, Tucker. I wasn't sure how you'd react. I was waiting until I thought it wouldn't break your heart." She rose and hugged him, drawing him farther into the room.

"Before today, I wasn't ready. If you'd asked me, I'd have said no." He sucked in a ragged breath. "But, that's my son. So full of life and pride. I'm proud of him. I should have watched this long ago. Mom's going to love this."

The men sat side by side on the couch to re-watch the video; their smiles grew each time through. Steph watched them heal together. Her broken heart mended, just a little, as joy overtook their sorrow.

"I want to tell you guys something." She waited until they'd watched the video four times before speaking. After a deep breath, she went on. "Elijah was a huge piece of my heart. He had pride and determination beyond anything I'd ever seen. He'd have gone a long way if not for the accident." Tears choked her words and she swallowed the lump in her throat. "I have money, not a lot, but enough to start a foundation for kids. I'm not sure what yet. But something to do with kids and this ranch. Something for healing and growing and missed opportunities."

She couldn't quite put her thoughts in order, so she blundered on. "I want to help kids in Elijah's memory. There's an idea nagging in the back of my mind. I can't quite focus on it, but it's there. I'd welcome any suggestions or thoughts. You guys knew him as well as I did. Tucker, for sure you knew him better. He was my student and my friend. He'd want to help other kids. You watched him helping his classmates with the guitar." She waved toward the screen.

Neither man spoke; they just looked thoughtful.

"He would want to help." Tucker stood and wandered around the room, stopping to run his finger down a picture of Steph and Elijah at a school barbeque. "I remember this."

"Maybe it could involve music?" Brett suggested. "He loved that guitar."

Steph laughed. "I know absolutely nothing about music. I don't play an instrument. I love to sing, it's just not my gift." She chuckled at her own lack of talent.

"With or without parents? Siblings?" Tucker asked.

"I don't know. I just saved some money for this project, but the idea isn't fully formed yet. I'm not going to rush into anything. There'll be tons of research into what to do, how to do it, if I can get any grants. That sort of thing. I just wanted you to know what I was thinking. Brett, you're creative and Tucker's a lawyer. I know kids. Maybe between the three of us, we can brainstorm an idea or two."

"I can have my charity organization help out."

"You've got a charity?" She stared at Brett. She thought she knew everything about him, apparently, she was wrong. How had he managed to keep it a secret from the press? He donated time and money to The Toronto SickKids Hospital as well as both the Alberta Children's Hospital in Calgary and the Stollery Children's Hospital in Edmonton. And, she'd read something once about donations to Ronald McDonald House Children's Charity, though details escaped her. As a fan, his generosity to children's organizations had appealed to her; but knowing he had a separate, private, charity, melted her heart.

It seemed like the more she learned about him, the deeper he wiggled into her heart. Yeah, he'd been irate when he'd learned of her role in Elijah's death; but he seemed to be moving beyond that.

Oh, stop it. Brett Wyatt is a superstar. He has no use or room in his life for a small-town girl like you. Back off and stop drooling over him. She snickered at her own mental gymnastics. She turned away before either man noticed her silly grin. She was entitled to her out-of-this-world fantasies, but she didn't need to share them with these two.

"Anyone for coffee? I can whip up a pot and bring it in here." Steph extended the offer to cover her thoughts.

"Double-double for me," Tucker agreed.

"And, I'll have black, one sugar. Please."

Steph bumped into a strange woman on her way to the kitchen. "Hi, I'm Stephanie Alexander. This is my place. Can I help you?"

The woman looked Steph up and down, taking in her fuzzy slippers, jeans, button-down plaid shirt and messy bun. She didn't say a word yet managed to dismiss Steph as if she were beneath her notice.

Steph stared back. The woman was tall, probably five-nine and barely weighed anything. The heaviest part of her were her enormous breasts. *Were they even real?* Stiletto heels, tight leather pants, low-cut, high-rising, sparkly top and dangling earrings like massive fishhooks. Her hair was cropped short, spiked up. The roots were blonde, the tips colored in a rainbow of hues. For a second, Steph wondered how she managed to get each tip different. Then, her attention flashed to those stilettos; they were floor wreckers for sure.

"How can I help you?"

The woman took a step forward. "I'm with Brett Wyatt, I have a reservation."

"Welcome to the Wild Rose Inn. I'll help you check in." She offered her hand, after a moment, she dropped it to her side. She'd met with this type before. Too good for the help. But, she was a guest, Brett's guest. His girlfriend? Her stomach and teeth clenched. She brushed her opinions and disappointment aside.

"Please come in. I'd appreciate it if you could refrain from wearing those heels on the hardwood. They're likely to leave scars."

The woman ignored her and stepped around Steph. "Where is Brett?"

Steph turned to follow her. "I'm sorry, I cannot divulge information on other guests, but if you'd like to check in, I'd be happy to assist you."

"Fine, let's get this over with. I was assured everything was taken care of. I should have known this bodunk place would be sub-par. I'd much rather have vacationed in New York; at least I'd have something to do, and room service." She sniffed disdainfully.

"This way, please." Steph led her mystery guest to the check-in desk. She must be Lola, Brett's band manager, but until she had proof of the woman's identity, she wasn't sharing one lick of information with her.

"I'll need some ID, please."

"I thought this was taken care of?" the blonde snapped.

The woman was as prickly as the multi-color porcupine she resembled. Steph hid her smile. "If, indeed, you are registered, we'll have you settled in no time."

Blondie dropped her enormous Gucci bag on the counter and rummaged through it. "Here." She snapped her driver's license on the counter and tapped her fingers impatiently.

Steph picked it up and looked between the picture and the woman several times with a frown on her face. "Yes, this does *seem* to be you. Let me check the book for your reservation." She flipped through her computer records despite knowing this woman, Lola, was with Brett.

"Can you hurry it up, I need a long soak in the tub. You do have bathtubs, don't you? Preferably a jet-tub."

"Yes, we have bathtubs. Unfortunately, the last room with a jetted tub is already taken, Miss Langtree. I expect a regular room will suffice?" The only room with a jetted tub was Brett's and she wasn't going to move him to accommodate this snippy woman.

She handed Lola a key. "Let me show you to your room. Do

you have any baggage?" She'd bet her life this princess had more than one kind of baggage.

"In my car. Out front. The Mercedes." She handed her keys to Steph. "You can bring my bags up and then move it to the parking garage. I'd like it washed and detailed, please."

Steph bit back a jolt of anger. She would not play slave to this woman, or any other. "I'm sorry, Miss Langtree, but we don't offer car detailing. I'd be happy to carry your bags and move your car to the parking pad, all parking is outdoors."

She tried to make small talk on the short trip upstairs, but Lola ignored her. Steph unlocked the room and gave her the usual spiel about meal times and amenities.

"I'm sorry, that won't work for me. I'll have my breakfast delivered to my room when I wake up at eleven-thirty."

"No, you won't. My apologies for the lack of amenities, but this is a small-town bed and breakfast, it isn't the New York Hilton. I'd be happy to save you a cold breakfast of fruit, yogurt and pastries. You can make your way to the kitchen when you're ready to eat. If you wish, bringing your meal back to your room is acceptable."

"I'd like to talk to the manager about that." Ice dripped from Lola's words and ignited a cold fury in Steph's blood.

"I am the manager." She kept her voice as sweet as possible. Dealing with this woman was going to kill her. She rarely had demanding guests, but she'd learned to treat them like recalcitrant children.

"Then I'd like to talk to the owner. Please." She sneered the last word.

"I am the owner. I'll take your requests under advisement." She paused, thinking. "Sorry, we cannot accommodate those requests at this time. Perhaps on your next stay?"

"I doubt there'll be a next stay. Now, where is Brett?" She looked around the room as if expecting to find him sitting there, waiting for her.

"Mr. Wyatt is in the entertainment room. Downstairs. You'll

find a map in the binder in your desk drawer. Please, enjoy your stay and let me know if you need anything."

"Extra pillows. Hypo-allergenic, please."

Steph bowed. "I'll see to it myself." She turned and headed downstairs. Lola slammed and locked the door behind her and followed hot on Steph's heels.

Brett stood at the base of the stairs, near the lobby. "Steph, we thought you were lost."

Lola pushed past Steph, nearly shoving her down the last few stairs. She raced across the small space and jumped at Brett, throwing her arms around his neck and her legs around his waist. He wrapped his arms around her and stumbled back half a step.

"Brett, darling. I missed you so much." She planted little kisses all over his face and neck.

Brett set her down and stepped away. He frowned at her. "Lola, I've asked you more than once to stop with the public displays of affection. They aren't professional."

"But, Brett, darling. I adore you and I can't resist you." She petted his arm. He shrugged her off. "We're good together."

Steph watched the display from the bottom step. Brett was having a fling with her? She didn't seem his type at all. She was all high-maintenance and he was helpful and accommodating. Weird combination. She shrugged the thought off. She had work to do.

"Miss Langtree, I'm bringing Mr. Wyatt coffee in the entertainment room, would you like anything?"

"A mimosa would be darling." She fiddled with her non-existent hair.

"I'm sorry, The Wild Rose Inn doesn't serve alcohol, though you are welcome to provide your own."

"Fine. I'll have a double, half-caf, soy latte with two shots of caramel."

"Lola." Brett's single word was sharp and chiding.

"Two creams and three sugars. Please. Whipped cream on top if you have it." There was enough drama in her voice to supply a stage company for a year.

Steph nodded and stepped around them toward the kitchen. Lola's complaints about the roads and primitive accommodations followed Steph into the kitchen. She forced herself not to slam the door shut to halt the string of inanities. The rich scent of fried beef, tomato and spices barely registered.

"Fudge, nuts and popcorn."

"Wow, you're in a mood." Penny turned from the stove to look at Steph. Her expression hovered somewhere between amusement and concern.

"Brett's band manager, Lola, just arrived. I've met princesses with less of an attitude. She's a pip." She sighed and removed the filter from the coffee pot and dumped the filter and grounds into the compost bin. "She wants breakfast in bed, her car detailed and mimosas. Can you imagine?"

Penny laughed and returned to stirring the pot of chili on the stove. "She's in for a rude awakening."

"And she was all over Brett like she wanted to eat him up and he barely objected." Steph slammed a tin of coffee on the counter and flipped the lip off.

"Jealous much?"

She pivoted to stare at her friend. "Not hardly."

"Liar. You're goo-goo eyes over him. Yeah, I know you'd never act on it, but you've got to admit he's one heck of a hunk. So sexy, hot and sweet. Mind you, he's got nothing on JT."

"I am not interested in Brett. Not now, not ever." She put a new filter in the pot and measured in the coffee. "Do you think they're a thing?"

"I thought you weren't interested?"

"I'm not. What's with you and JT? You two have been pretty tight the last few days." She didn't even pretend she wasn't trying to change the subject.

"Nice deflection. We just talk. JT's a nice guy. Single. We have a lot in common. Except, he loves to travel and I'm more a homebody."

"Sparks?" Steph laughed when Penny blushed bright red to the roots of her hair.

"Oh my gosh." She fanned her face. "You have no idea. And, I've never felt such an instant connection to anyone before. It's insane."

Steph switched on the industrial coffee brewer and embraced her friend. "Go carefully. He hangs out around concerts and big stars. He might not be all he seems. I don't want you to get hurt."

"No worries here. I'm not in a hurry to date anyone. He's just a nice guy and I'll enjoy talking to him while he's here."

"Just talking?" Steph nudged her friend. "I'll bet."

"I'm not giving it up until I meet the man I intend to marry. No fear of inappropriate behavior reflecting badly on the inn." Every ounce of frivolity was gone from Penny's demeanor. She was deadly serious. "You know how Mom was. I won't be like she was."

"I never met your mom before she passed on; but from what you said, I can paint a picture. No matter what you did, you could never be like her. It isn't in you. You're a good person and you need to stop thinking you'll end up like her."

"Thanks. It means a lot to hear you say that. Now finish what you're doing and get out of my kitchen. The rest of the staff will be here soon, and chaos will reign for hours. I won't have a minute to relax until dinner's been served."

A thermal carafe of coffee, cream and sugar cookies, joined chocolates and mugs on a pretty tea tray. Steph tossed on some spoons and napkins and lifted the heavy tray. "Grab the door for me, please."

Penny scurried over and opened the door. "I'll see you at dinner time."

"Thanks. Give me a shout if you need extra hands."

She dropped the tray off in the recreation room and headed for the door. The sight of Lola hanging on Brett's arm sickened her.

Bile rose in her throat. What did he see in her? She seemed so shallow.

"Wait," Brett called. "Aren't you joining us? I thought we were brainstorming."

"Perhaps later. I've got a ton of paperwork to do and I need to bring Miss Langtree's bags in. Thanks for the invitation."

"Oh, could you unpack my luggage and put it away? That would be darling."

Brett whirled round to stare at Lola. "No, she will not unpack your suitcases. She's not your maid. Fend for yourself for once."

"Technically, she is my maid." She wrinkled her nose and dipped her head to the left in defiance. "But fine, I'll unpack myself; but next time, we go someplace with service."

The woman was unbelievable. She had guts to spare. Steph hurried from the room and into her office and shut the door behind her. Just over two weeks remained in Brett's stay. She could get through this. Then, she was taking a vacation. Far away from country musicians and their staff, or groupies, or whoever Lola was.

CHAPTER 6

After ten days of living with Brett and his band, Steph was ready for a break. She paced impatiently back and forth between the front entry and the kitchen. Her cowboy boots tapped out a frenzied rhythm as she moved. There were a thousand things she'd rather be doing than taking Brett into town to run errands. Surely the man could send someone to do his chores. Tucker was more than capable, but Brett's friend and lawyer had other plans for the day and she knew what those plans were. The entire band and all the roadies were headed to a widened-out area of the slow-moving creek running through the ranch. Years ago, one of her relatives had created a swimming hole. As time passed, it had undergone upgrades.

The swimming hole was wide, and deep enough to swim without presenting too serious a hazard for young ones. There were now gravel shores as sand tended to wash away too easily. Benches and picnic tables in the shade and plenty of manicured grass provided space for lounging. The area was fenced off from the cattle to avoid cow patties where people wanted to go barefoot.

The day was a scorcher. Three in the afternoon and twenty-five degrees Celsius. Perfect day for playing in the water. Instead, she was headed to town with Brett, if he ever showed up. She wouldn't have gone swimming anyway. She usually sent one of the ranch hands to supervise, two if there were children going; but she avoided trips to town whenever she could and a teeny-tiny part of her resented not being invited to swim.

Whenever she went to town, she couldn't shake the feeling that people were staring at her, watching her and judging her for her past mistakes. Fame or infamy wasn't a pleasant thing to live with. Rather than stress herself, she reduced her trips to town to every ten days. She had accounts with the stores, and one of the hands picked up her orders.

Brett had two minutes to show up; if he didn't, the trip was off. He could take her pickup for all she cared. Town wasn't hard to find, just take the gravel road to the highway, turn left and keep on driving. Eventually, you'd end up in Okotoks. Brett had a smart-phone, she'd seen it. He could Google directions if he got lost.

She turned toward the stairs at the sound of boot steps descending. Dang. Freedom had been so close.

He paused at the base of the stairs, one hand on the railing, the other tucked into his front pocket. He looked like a model for a country magazine. What was she thinking? He'd been on more than one cover. He should be on a romance novel. Her heart went pit-a-pat and thundered into double beats. She took a slow, deep breath and calmed her nerves.

Yeah, she'd never get tired of seeing him in her house. Especially when he was looking every inch the sexy cowboy in his Wranglers, boots and button-down shirt. Too bad he was so wrapped up in his stage career and whatever he had going on with Lola. Although admittedly it seemed like Lola was far more into Brett than he was into Lola.

"Ready to go?" He flashed his patented grin and winked.

"At your command, superstar." His smile turned forced.

"Come on, Steph. Don't buy into the hype. That's my stage

persona, not the real me. I'm just a down-to-earth guy. Nothing special. I'm just a voice."

She paused at his words. Was his humble attitude real; or just another act? No way to know for sure unless she got to know him better. "Shall I drive or navigate while you drive?"

"I'm good if you prefer to drive. It'll allow me to enjoy the scenery."

They climbed into her navy 2002 Ford pickup and before she realized it they'd arrived. She waited in the lobby while he had a private meeting with the bank manager.

Twenty minutes later, they hit Walker's Country N' Western Wear and Lammle's for a bit of shopping.

"That's a lot of clothing," she teased.

"I like to look my best in concert. Stampede is special; so new boots, hat and clothing. What do you think of this shirt?" He held out a black, button-down shirt with white shoulders and epaulets.

"It's a bit flashy. It doesn't seem quite your style." She looked around. "What about this one?" She held up a two-toned blue and white shirt. The colors swirled together. It should have looked gaudy, but it was classy and elegant.

Brett wrinkled his nose. "I don't know."

"Come on, try it on. You don't have to buy it just because I like it."

He slipped into the change room with the shirt.

Steph tried on cowboy hats while she waited.

"I like that one." He pointed to her hat as he exited the booth. "It matches my show hat."

"Your show hat?" She studied his reflection in the mirror.

"I have my regular hats, like this one, and my show hats. They're a bit lighter weight. I have them custom made by Smithbilt Hats. The one you've got on is virtually the same hat." He ran his finger around the brim. "It looks good on you. You should get it. Better yet, let me buy it for you."

"No, thank you." She returned the hat to the rack and

wandered into the ladies' wear section. He followed but didn't press the issue.

"What about this style?" The petite blonde sales clerk held up a navy, snap-front shirt with white fringe.

"Oh darlin', I never wear snaps, and no self-respecting cowboy would be caught dead in fringe. It's a great color though." He winked. "I think I'll take this one instead. It's better on me than it was on the hanger. You were right, Steph."

"It does look good on you." She ran her hands over his shoulders and pivoted him around to get the full effect. "It's a perfect fit."

Brett changed into his own clothing and handed the shirt to the clerk. "We'll take this one, too." She grinned and gave him a flirty wink before hurrying off to the cash register.

"That's easy for you, isn't it?"

"What?"

"The flirting? Don't you worry you're leading them on? She's the third one today." Every interaction she'd witnessed was the same; people realized who he was and he charmed their socks off. Even the middle-aged male banker had been star-struck.

"I don't see the issue. I get great service and they get bragging rights, tips and autographs. It's a win-win really." He sounded genuinely puzzled

"I suppose, I hadn't seen it that way. Perhaps you're right."

"Wait until dinner. We'll get the best food and service."

What was he talking about? "Dinner?"

"I've made a reservation for a private room in a local restaurant. I'm giving you the night off." He grinned.

"I have to be back to help with dinner at the Inn."

"All taken care of. I talked to Penny. She'll handle everything. I worked my charm on her." He paused. "Okay, I had JT work his charm on her. She's immune to me." He shook his head and laughed.

They left the shop with another bundle of shopping bags and three hat boxes. Brett wore a brand-new Stetson and the cashier clutched his old, autographed one to her chest and grinned like a fool. Outside, they paused while he signed autographs and talked to a few people.

The crowd grew and swelled again. With every increase in fans, her heartrate accelerated. Sooner or later, somebody was going to notice her. She shrank inside herself and kept her head tipped down. The first opportunity she got, she slid into the truck and closed the door behind her. It wasn't much, but the security of having a wall between her and all those people gave a small measure of relief and eased the tightening in her chest.

How did he do it? He adored his fans as much as they loved him. Everyone was polite and patient as he smiled, chatted and signed whatever paper was thrust under his nose. He gave two small girls quick piggy-back rides. The crowd applauded as he galloped up and down the sidewalk. The tots giggled in delight when he handed them to their mothers.

At last, he held up a hand. "Folks, I'd love to stay and chat with you, but I've got an important appointment. Have a great day." He waved and climbed into the truck. The crowd backed off leaving more than enough room for them to drive away.

"You're good with people." She glanced at him out of the corner of her eye.

"I try to be. Today was easy. Sometimes, after a concert, when I'm exhausted, they start shoving and shouting. It's hard to keep up a happy face then. Typically, they're polite and patient." He shrugged. "All part of the gig."

"And you love it."

"Guilty. I love the fans and the spotlight as much as I love the music." He rubbed his hands briskly together. "Now, a quick stop at Smithbilt Hats and Alberta Boot Company and then we'll have just enough time to get to the tower."

"The Calgary Tower?" What was he thinking? You took dates to the tower, not your innkeeper. "But—"

"Hush. Stop fretting. I love the view from up there. I eat there every time I'm in Calgary. I made reservations. Come, eat with me. Don't make me eat alone. The view's too beautiful to waste."

Reluctantly, she agreed. With luck, the tower wouldn't be overly busy since it was Wednesday. Friday would have been a nightmare. She followed his instructions to the parkade where a private, plain-clothes security guard met them and escorted them past the tower line-up and straight to the elevator. Alone in the elevator, she watched the digital scene showing off Calgary's skyline. Brett nudged her with his elbow. "See, there are perks to being famous. No need to wait in line."

The hostess greeted them with a star-stuck grin and led them to a table for six, set with only two place settings and surrounded by privacy screens on two sides. "As ordered, Mr. Wyatt. You'll be able to enjoy your evening without feeling like you're on display."

"Thanks, darlin'." He winked and handed her a generous tip. Her face went pink and she giggled before leaving them alone.

Steph grimaced. The man threw money around like it was water.

"I saw that frown. Want to tell me what it's all about?" He shuffled his silverware to the side and leaned forward, elbows resting on the table.

"Nothing." She turned her attention from his penetrating gaze and stared out the window of the revolving restaurant. "It's beautiful out there." She gestured toward the Saddledome, Calgary's aging hockey arena, as it rolled into view.

"How about some honesty?"

She turned toward him. His brows were scrunched together, and his hands were clasped together on the table. He met her gaze without looking away. Something in his eyes radiated sincerity and concern. She thought for a moment, considering her options. She owed him nothing. Being famous didn't make him privy to her innermost thoughts.

"You spend money like water and flash yourself around

expecting to get everything you want. At the same time, you're not vain, you're almost humble. I don't get it."

He nodded thoughtfully. "Fans are my bread and butter. Like guests are yours. If I treat them right, they're happy. They might come to another concert, or buy another CD; just like your guests will return if they're satisfied. It's the same. Business."

"No." She shook her head. "It's more... you glow when you talk to them. Their adoration keeps you alive. You thrive on it."

"I suppose I do."

"Excuse me." The waitress returned, cell phone in hand. "Do you think I could get a picture of you guys? It's okay if you say no."

Brett looked at Steph. She shook her head slightly. He replied with a miniature nod. "How about if my friend takes a picture of you and me instead?"

"Oh, gosh! Really? You'd do that for me?" She squealed and vibrated in place.

"Sure." He pushed back his chair and stood beside her. "Hand my friend your phone." He slung one arm casually over the girl's shoulder as Steph took the phone. "Say cheese."

Steph snapped off a couple pictures. Brett dropped his hat on the girl's head and she snapped a few more.

"Gosh. Golly. My friends aren't going to believe this."

"You've got photo proof." Brett laughed. "Tell you what, if you let us eat in peace, I'll even sign an autograph for you. When we're finished." He winked. Again. She dimpled and left them alone. He dropped his hat onto a spare chair.

Once they'd placed their orders and were sipping a lovely Riesling, Brett patted her hand where it lay on the table alongside her glass.

"It really bothers you, doesn't it?"

"Yes, and no. You charm them so easily, and they fall for your handsome, country-boy charm. It's—I don't know what it is. Dishonest?"

"You think I'm handsome and charming?" Laugh lines appeared at the corner of his eyes.

"That was your take-away? What about the dishonest part?" She refused to be taken in by his smile and boyish delight.

"I'm not dishonest. I believe in telling the truth. I might tell a white lie now and then, but only to avoid hurting someone. Like when someone asks me how lovely their newborn is; every newborn is red and wrinkled and u-ugly. But, there's no way I'd ever tell the baby's parents their child was less than perfect. As for my charm, it's just who I am. I treat people well and in exchange I expect them to treat me well. If an extra smile or autograph gets me a new fan or some private time, I consider it a fair trade."

"I don't know..." She fiddled with her napkin and sipped her wine. After a moment of staring out the window and watching the Saddledome and Bow Tower slide past, she turned toward him. Their gazes met with an electric charge that jolted all the way down to her toes curling them in her cowboy boots.

Wowsers!

She knotted her hands together on top of the table to keep them from reaching out and stroking him. How did one look have such power?

He reached out and cupped her clenched fingers in his. "It's important to me you understand this. I admit that sometimes, I pour on a bit of extra charm in exchange for unspecified favors."

Her eyebrow tilted upward.

"Not *that*." He laughed. "I've never done that with anyone I wasn't in a serious relationship with, no matter what the tabloids say." The corners of his mouth twitched in a grin. "If I spent as much time in bed with starlets and models as the tabloids claim, I wouldn't have time to perform in concert." He sobered. "I know a lot of stars, some way more famous than I am who don't hesitate to use their fame in unscrupulous ways. I won't. But, in all honesty, I don't use any more charm now that I'm famous than I did when I was a kid in a garage band. It isn't in me." He leaned back and sighed. "I can see you're not convinced."

He was right. Sure, he had the words down, like a rehearsed speech and they rang true. But if he was being honest, he might just be too good to be true. "And Lola?"

"Lola is my band manager. She keeps track of equipment and keeps the roadies in check. I'm not in a relationship with her, although I'm certain she wants to be."

"Yeah, I can see you're not in anything with her. I saw the way you greeted her when she arrived." Oh, sweet heaven; why had she gone and said that?

"No, you saw the way she greeted me. There's a world of difference. Are you jealous?"

"No!" Heat rose in her face. She snatched up her wine and downed it in two swallows.

"Keep drinking like that and you'll be drunker than the parson's pig."

"The what?" She nearly laughed wine out her nose.

"The parson's pig. My grandfather's expression. I asked for an explanation more than once. Every time I asked, I got a different answer."

She laughed, tension flowed from her shoulders.

"The thing about Lola is that she's good at her job. I've had three band managers, and she's better than any of them by a factor of four. She's outrageous, demanding and over the top."

"You think?" Sarcasm dripped like treacle from her words.

"Tsk. Let me finish. Her attitude and princess complex gets things done. I don't know how, but it does. She's attractive and that helps control the boys. They're men with men's urges which drive them to please her." He shrugged. "But, I swear to God, I've never slept with her, kissed her or anything else and I never will. She's not my type. She's way too high maintenance for me. Someday, when I'm looking to settle down, I want someone like you."

Her heart jumped in her chest. Like her? No way!

"I want someone down to earth, unmoved by my fame. My ideal woman is level-headed, calm, organized and great with kids." After a short thoughtful pause, he continued. "She'll be independent but fun and loving. She'll care for others and have a generous heart, and she'll have the courage to stand up for what she wants and to put me in my place when I need it."

"Wow, that's quite a list."

"It is. I never really thought about it before this conversation. I just know I'll recognize her when I see her."

A weird emotion raced across his face. It was there and gone before she could identify it. She pondered his expression and his list. She had a lot of those qualities. Too bad she couldn't see herself with a man too wrapped up in his career to leave time for anything else.

"I hope you find what you're looking for." The words came out stiff, but she meant them. They'd only known each other for a few days, and their friendship had run the gamut of ups and downs; but she liked him. A lot. Perhaps too much. She wanted him to be happy and for all his protestations that the concert scene was the perfect life, she wondered if he realized the wistfulness in his voice when he talked of his ideal woman. Perhaps his life wasn't all he'd hoped it would be.

"And you? What are you looking for in a man?"

"This is an unusual conversation for people who don't know each other well."

"And you're avoiding the question." He refilled their wine glasses. "This is just a chat between friends. Friends who I hope are comfortable enough with each other to talk honestly."

"Aren't you worried I'll run to the tabloids with your revelations?" She wrinkled her nose.

"Honestly? Not one bit. Sure, Tucker recommended you as honest and discreet, but I'd trust you anyway. There's an integrity in you the whole world can see. And you reinforced that when you refused to tell Lola where I was until she proved her identity.

So, tell me, Stephanie Alexander; what do you look for in a man?"

"Nothing. I stopped looking a long time ago. I've had serious relationships, some good, some not so good and I've decided to let fate take control and bring the right guy to me. You said it yourself, I'll know the right person when I find him." *And it won't be you, no matter how much cowboy charm and handsome good looks you possess.*

"Okay. Not looking doesn't mean there isn't a list. All women have lists."

The waiter slid their plates in front of them and checked if they needed anything else. Steph studied the mushroom-topped steak, garlic mashed potatoes and asparagus on her plate. It looked divine and smelled delicious. Her appetite fled. How did one even generate a list, let alone reveal it to the man who might just fit the traits she desired. They ate a few bites before she responded.

"My list is simple. Caring, honest, and a sense of humor. He'll be a hard worker and place his family above everything else. He'll care for his community and he'll adore me." She nibbled at her potatoes.

"And what does this paragon of virtue look like?" His voice landed somewhere between laughter and serious inquiry.

"I have no freaking idea. I haven't met him yet. Looks aren't important to me. Sure, they play a factor in first impressions, but beauty fades; what's inside doesn't. I'm looking for a man who's beautiful inside and devoted to his family; as in me and our children."

"You want children?"

"Don't you?"

"I've never really thought about it. After losing Elijah, I'm not sure I could take the risk."

"Love is always a risk. I'd rather love and lose than never love at all. I'll take motherhood with all its risks. The pure joy of family would outweigh any pain." Conviction rang in her voice; she'd revealed more than she intended. Something about Brett made her say things better left unspoken. They ate in silence for a few moments.

"I hear you playing a lot, you practice for hours when you aren't outside walking around or kibitzing with the guys. I never hear you singing. Don't you need to keep your voice tuned up, too?"

He set down his fork and looked at her, his expression flat and unreadable. "I told you I needed to rest my voice. It's killing me not to sing. But I've overworked my vocal cords and need to rest them as much as possible. Talking is fine, but no shouting or singing. A couple weeks ago in a concert, my voice cracked. Three nights later, it cracked again. I'm on singing sabbatical. I'm saving my voice to sing at the Stampede. It's a hard gig to get. We've been pre-booked for three years. I'd hate to cancel and risk not getting the chance to play there again. We've rescheduled the rest of the tour. One last group of concerts and I'm homebound for a couple months. Maybe longer. If I damage my vocal cords permanently, my career will be over. I'll have nothing left."

His face was white, his entire body tense. Fear, near panic, radiated off him in waves. He leaned back in his chair, arms crossed over his chest. Empathy clutched at her heart and her body echoed his tension. God, she knew the pain of losing your passion all too well. She'd barely recovered when she'd lost teaching. Sometimes, she felt like she hadn't recovered at all.

Stretching out as far as she could, she reached over the table and patted his arm. "Good thing you're resting your voice then." She smiled a little sadly. "I'd be lost without another Brett Wyatt album to murder."

He let out a sharp bark of laughter. "Perhaps I should avoid recording again and save the world some broken eardrums."

She laughed along with him. Her singing was brutal, she knew it and sang anyway. She watched the tension ebb from his shoulders. He picked up his fork and finished his meal.

"Want to go for a walk? I know a great place between here and home."

"No dessert? No after-dinner cocktail?"

"I'm stuffed. But, if I get hungry on the way home, I'll let you buy me a treat." She stuck out her hand.

"Deal." They shook to seal the deal and he texted his security guard to escort them out.

"Do you do that often? Have a personal guard, I mean? Will he walk with us, too?" She gave him a puzzled look. *Wouldn't that spoil the mood? Okay, so there was no mood.* They were friends, but she wanted to indulge in the fantasy, just a little, while she had the chance. Before she knew it, he'd be gone and all she'd have left was a few memories of good times and a wicked argument about Elijah which had ended up healing them both.

CHAPTER 7

Brett hopped out of the truck half a second after Steph. "Are you sure the owner won't mind us wandering around on his property? I know this is close to your place, but what if he starts shooting at us for trespassing?"

"Relax. She won't mind a bit. I guarantee nobody will be shooting at you. Grab your jacket." She slung her jacket and a small canvas bag over her shoulder, locked the truck and wandered down a goat-path of a road toward the trees. He jogged to keep up.

"Are you sure I'm safe? You're not trying to do away with me, are you?" His voice rose plaintively on the last word. He wasn't in the least bit worried about his safety; but being arrested for trespassing was sure to make the papers. He could do without the publicity.

Whoa!

He stopped dead. When had he ever minded the publicity? If he was in the public spotlight, his fans couldn't forget about him. Even when the tabloids mangled the facts, it was beneficial. He wasn't tiring of his adoring fans, was he? He shook his head and hurried to catch up before Steph disappeared from sight. Jogging in cowboy boots was no easy feat. Doable yes, easy no. He did his running on the treadmill, although lately he'd taken to walking around the ranch. He worried the labored breathing of running might not be good for his throat. It probably wouldn't damage anything, but why take the risk with his livelihood?

Ahead of him, Steph bent over at the waist to pick something up off the ground. He stumbled and nearly fell. Dear God! The woman had the nicest backside. Holy Hanna. How could he have forgotten after seeing her dance? His libido kicked into overdrive. Oh yeah, he was in trouble, big trouble. Maybe a little *exercise* wouldn't be so bad after all. It might be worth the risk.

"You coming or what?" she teased.

It took every bit of his willpower not to make an off-color response. "Where are we headed?"

"Ah, superstar, just wait and see. Patience is a virtue, you know. It's not far, only about a thousand yards." Her voice lilted with laughter.

He shifted a bit to loosen the sudden tightening in his jeans. This was not happening. Not to him. Nope. No frickin' way. He was always in control of his physical responses. Always. "A thousand yards? That's a kilometer!" He feigned indignation just to make her laugh again; he must be a glutton for punishment.

"Big fat baby, you'll live." She trotted off leaving him gaping behind. She was up to something. He hurried to catch up. She disappeared around a bend and he doubled his pace. Rounding the corner, he nearly rammed into her spreading a blanket on the grass beside an enormous natural pool. She'd discarded the canvas bag and her jacket on the grass.

"Isn't it going to be dark soon?" He looked around the dim clearing, trying to gauge the time. It was so hard to pinpoint the exact hour when dusk was falling and daylight fading. Probably an hour until full dark, or less, unless he missed his guess.

"Yup. Tonight's the full moon. It'll be as bright as daylight in twenty minutes." She flopped onto the blanket and lay back staring at the sky, a huge smile on her face. "I don't get out here nearly enough. This is what you missed going into town instead of swimming with everyone else."

"I didn't miss a damned thing. I had a great day and dinner with a beautiful woman." He settled beside her, legs stretched out in front of him and leaned back on his arms. He faced her, his knees near her head, his boots just off the blanket. He had a perfect view of the stream and her pretty face. She was so relaxed, so peaceful. Entirely different from the nearly invisible tension she carried in her shoulders all day.

Being in town bothered her. He liked her better this way; calm, and relaxed, with her body stretched out. He blocked any intimate thoughts; he barely had his last unanticipated reaction under control. Damn. Just thinking about it provoked a new result. He shifted one leg to block her view of his vitals and focused his attention on the water.

"Wait? This is your land?"

"It is." She chuckled. "Had you going for a minute there. You thought you'd get a load of rock salt in the fanny. Didn't you?"

"Do people even do that? Do they really load shotguns with salt instead of actual ammunition?"

"You better believe they do. It's a great way to scare off neighbors' dogs who keep coming around. Shoot away from them and the noise scares them off. Nobody gets hurt, the dog leaves and there are no pellets left behind, just a bit of salt to wash away in the next rain."

"I don't think I'd ever get used to rural life. I like the city and the protection of a building with a doorman and a guard."

"Ew." She wrinkled up her nose and he laughed. "I can't imagine. All the smog and being trapped inside. All the people. No, thank you. I'll take the solitude of the country any day. I don't miss the city at all." She paused. "Not true, I miss teaching. But I'm working on that."

"It bothers you to be in public, doesn't it?"

"Somewhat. Not as much as it used to. Right after the accident,

I couldn't even step foot outside my house without being assaulted by reporters. I finally came home to hide."

The sadness in her voice made his heart ache. He cleared his throat. "Is that what you're doing? Hiding? Surely it's blown over by now?" Conflicting thoughts ran through his head. Why did people attack like a pack of rabid animals and destroy each other? Before today, he never considered what the press was really like. When he was in public, he was fair game and he rarely had his privacy intruded upon, not like the media had done with Steph.

He'd done some internet searching last night and they'd crucified her after the accident. Huge destructive, damaging headlines declaring her guilt. Their accusations had no basis; but the headlines declared "Local Teacher Lets Student Drown." Later, when the dust settled and Tucker had won her compensation, their retractions had been nothing more than a tiny piece in a back section, unlikely to be seen by many people. As business practices went, the entire episode had been sketchy at best. No wonder she was gun shy.

"I'm not hiding, not exactly; but I refuse to subject myself to that kind of scrutiny again. I'm content in my small part of the world. Okotoks is big, but not city big. I love my new life, even if I miss parts of the old. I'll never understand how you can live in the spotlight."

Her comment rattled around in his brain and incited introspection. What did he get from being in the spotlight. Money? Sure, but he had more than enough to last a lifetime. Adoration? He had a great relationship with his fans. Unable to come to a firm rationalization, he avoided thinking about it, and pushed it to the rear of his brain.

He turned his attention to Steph. She'd pulled off her boots and rolled up her jeans. "I'm going to test the water? You coming?"

"It's getting kind of dark."

"Are you afraid of the dark?" She jumped to her feet with a giggle.

He had a perfect view of the top of her breasts when she bent to rummage through her canvas bag. She extracted a lantern and tossed it to him.

"Here, city boy. It's crank operated. Crank it up so you're not afraid." Sarcasm dripped from her voice.

He discarded the lightweight lamp and shed his boots in seconds. "I'll get you for that comment."

She raced toward the water; he leaped to his feet and followed her. She speed-minced her way over the gravel and into the creek. He only paused long enough to toss his cell phone and wallet on the shore before going in after her. The gravel bank was primarily rounded stone, but although it was painful to run over, it didn't slow him a bit.

She turned around and kicked water at him, laughing like a schoolgirl. The full moon was rising over the field behind her, throwing her into silhouette. Water droplets turned from black to sparkling silver in the moonlight. He froze in place, taking it all in, capturing one of the most beautiful sights he'd ever seen. She twirled and spun in the water, a dancer's silhouette of passion and joy.

His chest went tight with the need to kiss her, to absorb her passion and delight and make it his own. He stepped toward her, one arm reaching out. She slapped hands with him as she spun round and wiggling ferociously, she stepped farther and farther away.

Drawn like metal filings to a magnet, he followed, helpless to stop himself. Icy water pelted him in the face as she spun again, one foot raised to spray him over and over as she went around and around like a ballerina; her leg oscillating in and out of the water with each revolution. Drenched to the skin, he lunged forward to grasp her by the waist.

She tugged against his light grasp and they tumbled, together, into the calf-deep water. He rolled to pull her from beneath him, his head going under, the chill water stealing his breath. Crushed by panic for her safety, he struggled to sit. She surfaced from the water like a siren, flinging her long hair over and behind her head with her hands, her face wreathed in an enormous smile, laughter spilling from her lips.

Damn.

He still held her waist and somehow, thank the heavens, she'd ended up straddling his lap. Her joy and happiness captivated him, stealing his breath. He leaned in, slowly, and brushed his lips against hers. She was hot against the chill air; she tasted of the peppermint she'd eaten in the truck. She smelled like fresh air and sunshine and moonlight and romance. He kissed her again. Deeper, longer.

She leaned back and whispered, "This is such a bad idea."

His hands fell from her waist and he leaned away. He wouldn't push this instant of flaring passion. She hadn't objected to his kisses, which wasn't the same as sharing his feelings.

"Oh, to heck with it." She laughed and cupped his face in her hands and yanked him forward, taking his lips with hers. Heat furled in his belly and rushed through his body and lodged in his throbbing groin. Even his sodden jeans didn't bank the heat.

Their tongues danced and tangled. Advanced and retreated. He gripped her hips with his hands to keep them from roaming places he had no right to explore. Still, she kissed him. Giving and taking. He returned her affections with a fervor and tenderness he'd never known. Her hands slid down his face to his neck, warm and enticing against his chilled skin. His hands slipped upward, goosebumps rose on her skin beneath her untucked shirt.

"Wait. Stop." His words blurred against her lips. "Let's get out of this water before we freeze to death." He eased her to the side and stood, grasping her hand. He pulled her upward, and laughing they stumbled toward shore.

He embraced her, wrapping her in his arms to warm them both before starting to unbutton her shirt. She went rigid in his arms.

"Relax, I'm just getting rid of these wet clothes. The blanket will dry you off." She nodded her acquiescence. He fumbled to push the uncooperative buttons through the sodden fabric. He freed one button after another until her shirt hung open, clinging to the edges of her bare breasts. Sweet heaven, she was braless. He'd had no idea. Thank God, or he'd have had a hard-on all day.

He grabbed the blanket and swung it around her shoulders and held it there while she slipped out of her shirt and jeans. She stumbled around, dancing, laughing and shaking her legs to shed her sodden jeans. "Hold still." Kneeling in front of her, he grasped the waist of her jeans and inched them down her legs. Hot pink lace panties slid into view and threatened to cling to the jeans.

He grasped the lace with two fingers and used his free hand to get rid of the jeans. The image of her standing in the bright moonlight, clad in only pink lace and a blanket, burned into his brain. He'd never forget that vision. So hot, so sexy, so goddamn beautiful. He grasped two corners of the blanket and dried her briskly. He stood, spun her around and handed her the jacket she'd discarded earlier. The blanket dropped and she stood, her back to him, nearly naked. Dear lord she was breathtaking. He was doomed.

He turned away and shed his socks and jeans, discarding them on the ground. His shirt followed in short order. She made a small sound, somewhere between a sigh and a gasp. He glanced over his shoulder at her. She stared, open-mouthed, at his backside.

"Can I have the blanket?" He couldn't keep the laughter from his voice.

"What? Oh. Yeah." She stepped forward and wrapped it around his shoulders as he turned toward her. Copying his earlier actions, she dried him with the blanket. Each stroke against his cold, oversensitive skin was torture. He heated fast. Too fast. Blood rushed to every place she touched and to some she didn't.

She bent to towel his legs and he halted her with a hand on her shoulder. "I've got this." She stepped away, a small frown on her face.

"But—"

"No buts, I can do it." He wrapped the blanket around his waist and bent to finish drying. He turned his head and discovered he had a perfect view of the front of those damned panties. For the hundredth time that day, his disobedient cock twitched to life. He tried to look away. He tried with everything he had. But the naked skin between her panties and the hem of her denim jacket called to him and when her hand splayed across her belly, he nearly lost his mind.

"Son of a…" he whispered.

"Are you okay?" Her icy hand landed on his shoulder. It burned like a fiery brand.

"Fine," he choked the word out. "We better get to the truck and warm up."

"Are you sure?" She stepped forward and brushed her lips across his cheek and then against his mouth.

"Hell no!" He cupped her head and drew her closer to deepen the kiss. They kissed for a moment, or was it an hour? He lost track of time and everything else except the delicious, delirious taste of her. Breathless, he pulled back. "Come on, let's get to the truck before I do something crazy we'll both end up regretting."

She bit her lip in indecision and he nearly went for another taste.

"Damn, woman. You're driving me out of my mind. Come on." They struggled into their boots. Her socks made it easier, his damp, naked feet refused to slide inside his. Eventually, he had them on. One brief kiss and he turned her in the direction of the truck and scooped up his wallet and phone. He passed them to her and bundled up the wet clothing. With one hand clutching the blanket around his waist he smiled at her. "Grab the stuff."

She grabbed the lantern and bag and rummaged around until she produced the truck keys with a triumphant smile. "Race ya!"

She took off at a run her jacket flapping in the wind.

Cowboy boots, pink lace panties and a denim jacket disappearing in the distance was the sexiest thing he'd ever seen. He hightailed it after her, his laugh echoing in the night.

∼

THE TRUCK HEATER started pumping out heat immediately, warming their damp bodies. It was a short drive to the house, and Steph nearly stopped the truck half a dozen times for another kiss. She snuck a side-glance at Brett. The blanket had dropped to his waist and he sat there, Brett-freaking-Wyatt, country music superstar, sat there, in her truck, gloriously half-naked. Solid biceps, muscular forearms and large competent hands. She'd seen what those hands were capable of with a guitar. It didn't take much imagination to translate that to something more personal. Strong shoulders, flat abs, there wasn't an inch of him she didn't want to explore with her hands or her tongue. Sweet heaven, just being beside him was arousing. She breathed deeply. Soft musk, citrus and outdoors. Oh yeah, the man was wreaking havoc on her equilibrium and she didn't mind one bit. There was no way she'd ever forget this moment, or the kiss they'd shared.

He'd curled her toes. Kissing wasn't something she did often, and kissing virtual strangers never happened, but wow! Brett Wyatt could kiss. She wanted, needed, another; even if she knew she couldn't go there again.

Keeping her eyes on the road, and off him, was the toughest thing she'd attempted in ages. Admittedly, she wasn't entirely successful, but she got them to the house safely. Before she hopped out of the truck, she placed her hand on his forearm. His skin twitched under her touch. Dang. She swallowed hard. So soft, so firm, so masculine. Until this moment, she'd been unaware of how much she missed being part of a couple since her disastrous breakup in the aftermath of Elijah's death.

"Thanks for today. It was nice to get out, I really enjoyed myself."

"Thank you. I have to admit, it was nice to be out without having to hide behind my public persona. But now, I need to get inside and find some dry clothing. This blanket is stylish but doesn't quite fit my image." He slid out of the truck as he spoke and swiveled his hips like a hula dancer, setting the blanket swaying back and forth.

A bubble of laughter escaped her lips and she slapped her hand over her mouth to keep from giggling aloud. Brett smirked and exaggerated his motions. Laughing like idiots, they stumbled into the house arm in arm.

"Well, isn't this cozy?" Derision dripped from Lola's voice.

"Miss Langtree. You're up late. Did you need something?" Steph grabbed Brett around the waist with a winning smile. It was mean, but she exerted her will as if he belonged to her. Lola scowled and Steph turned to the boot jack to remove her boots.

"I need to talk to Brett, not that it's any of your concern. Business matters. But I see he's been otherwise occupied." She tsked. "Really Brett, you left to run a few errands and ended up being out half the night with some local and you come home half-naked. The press will have a field day with this."

"Drop it, Lola." Brett kicked off his boots and set them alongside Steph's. "First, I can do whatever I choose. Second, I don't answer to you, you answer to me. Third, the press isn't here. And fourth, it's none of your damned business. You manage the roadies. JT is my manager and PR person. Back off."

"I need to talk to you," she reiterated. "I stayed up waiting for you, worried half out of my head and you come home like this."

Steph's temperature spiked with every word out of Lola's mouth. She bit the inside of her cheek until she tasted blood. She wouldn't dignify the thinly veiled accusations with a response. "Was there anything I could get either of you before I turn in?" She banked the urge to race up the stairs and hide in her room. This woman would not cow her into submission. They'd done nothing wrong. Dinner and a splash in the creek.

"I'm fine. We're fine. Thank you." His voice was soft, its deep silky tones slid over her skin like warm honey.

"I need herbal tea." Lola's tone grated on Steph's nerves like gravel in an open wound.

"She's fine. She can make her own tea. Good night, Steph." In three short sentences, his tone went from snapping to kind.

"All right, then. I'll just take those wet clothes and toss them in the dryer." She held out her hands for the dripping bundle clenched in Brett's fist. "Buzz me with the intercom on the check-in desk if you need anything. Good night. I'll see you both at breakfast."

Lola opened her mouth and snapped it shut at Brett's quelling look.

"Good night." He repeated, handing her the clothing.

Their fingers brushed as she grabbed the bundle. Sparks jumped from his hand to hers and she fumbled with the clothing. Clutching it to her chest, she walked away with as much dignity as she could muster clad only in panties, socks and a jean jacket.

She could have walked past Lola and up the main stair. Instead, she detoured through the kitchen and took the back stairs up. It gave her the satisfaction of turning her back on Lola's unpleasant and baseless accusations.

∽

BRETT DIDN'T TURN to watch Steph walk away. He couldn't. No way could he see her delicious backside retreating and not chase after her. With effort, he turned his mind to Lola. "Have you lost your mind?" Brett hissed when the kitchen door closed behind Steph. "Don't ever act like that again, or you're fired."

"Come on, Brett, I've saved you from over-zealous fans before. It's part of my gig." She sidled up to him and pressed her hand on his chest. "You do look damn nice half-naked, no wonder she's having trouble keeping her hands off you. Besides, you and I'd be great together."

What the hell? He stepped back and her hand fell away. Once, long ago they'd been fast friends, she'd been manager of the first band who'd hired him to fill in for a missing band member. They'd spent one night together, nothing more. Honestly, there wasn't any real chemistry between them. They'd struck up a friendship and started working together. She'd changed lately, and not for the better.

"Last warning. You and I aren't starting anything. Ever. And, strap on your best manners and start acting like a civilized human being before you make me do something I won't regret."

"But—" She reached toward him again.

"No buts. Back off. Leave Steph alone."

Her glare would have cut stone, but she didn't scare him, nor did her anger move him. All he felt was pity with a tinge of remorse. He should have called her on her bad behavior long before now.

CHAPTER 8

On any other day, six a.m. wouldn't be a problem; but after spending half the night pacing her bedroom, reviewing her evening with Brett and the embarrassing aftermath with Lola, Steph was beyond exhausted. Less than an hour's sleep wasn't enough to function on. She stumbled down to the kitchen and made herself a coffee. She hated espresso but she needed the caffeine hit. Three shots with three teaspoons of sugar and a cup of milk was like drinking syrup, but she gagged half of it down and popped some bread in for the toast she'd need to absorb the coffee.

"Well, look at you, you look like hell," Lola sneered from the doorway. She stood there, tall and proud. Her left hand on her hip, her breasts and chin thrust forward. Her dress was black and silky, more an evening dress than a summer frock. Her makeup and hair were perfect. Her eyes squinted together and her smile was as forced as Steph's, but she was still beautiful. How did anyone look so good this early in the morning?

Steph took a deep breath. She didn't need this crap. Not now, not ever. Lola had a knack for making her feel insignificant. There was nothing to gain by engaging in a verbal war with this woman. Steph mentally strapped on her adult panties and pasted on a smile.

"Good morning, Miss Langtree. You're up early. Would you like coffee or an early breakfast?"

"No." She sashayed closer until it was all Steph could do to remain still and not retreat to regain her personal space. It seemed intimidation was this morning's game. "I'm here to talk."

Steph waved toward the staff table. Her toast popped and she jumped at the sound. "Please, have a seat. I'll just butter my toast and join you." Dang, it was overdone, just verging on burnt, she should have been watching it. The toaster rarely popped at the right time. She buttered it anyway.

Half a minute later they sat at the table like two boxers facing off in the ring before a title fight. "What would you like to talk about?" She didn't want to hear this. Her guts clenched. Feigning unconcern, she nibbled at her toast then sipped her coffee.

Lola slapped her palms on the table. "Listen to me. It's my job to keep scheming women away from Brett. So, whatever your plans for him, drop them now. You're a dalliance, a fling at best. When we leave, he'll be done with you and you'll never hear from him again. If you try to contact him, his lawyer will be all over you."

Steph stifled a smile. His lawyer, Tucker, was her dear friend. But was she really only a flirtation? Last night the attraction between her and Brett had felt like more. Their friendship was slowly morphing into something else. At least she thought it was. Was she wrong? They'd spent hours together since he had arrived and she wanted more. She wasn't expecting hearts and flowers, but deeper friendship didn't seem out of the question.

"I'll tell you what." She smiled sweetly at Lola. "When Brett tells me to leave him alone, I'll do it without hesitation. No ifs, ands, buts or complaints."

Lola leaned over the table, obviously trying to intimidate her. Steph sipped her coffee, set the mug down and met her angry gaze without flinching.

"Brett and I are dating. Back away from my man; or you'll regret it."

Steph leaned back in her chair and lightly scratched her chin, pretending to consider the threat. Threats were nothing new to her, she'd faced off against more than one angry parent in her teaching days. She wasn't easily intimidated anymore. "I'll take your suggestion under advisement."

There was a whisper of sound in the doorway, she flicked her eyes up and then returned her attention to Lola. "The Wild Rose Inn is happy to consider our guests' requests and suggestions."

"This isn't a suggestion." She spit the words through gritted teeth. "Brett and I want you to stop chasing him. Leave him alone."

"Indeed." Brett stood in the doorway, cowboy hat slung low, travel mug in hand. Warmth rushed to her face and diffused through her body. Dang man heated her up with just a look.

"Good morning, Mr. Wyatt. You look like you need a coffee."

"I believe I've asked you repeatedly to call me Brett." His smile warmed her to her toes and chased off any lingering chill from Lola's not-so-subtle threats. The man was glorious in his western wear and hat. His smile could turn any woman to mush and she was no exception.

"Good morning, Brett." She slid from behind the table and strolled over to him. "Coffee?" She did call him Brett, in private. In public, she tried to keep it formal.

"Please. Strong and black would be lovely." He slid into the chair she'd vacated. "Morning, Lola. You're up uncharacteristically early." His sweet tone was belied by his thunderous expression.

"I know you're an early riser. I thought I'd join you on your morning walk."

"In that dress and those heels? You'd break your ankle; and stop wearing your stilettos on Steph's hardwood floors. I'm not asking, I'm telling you. Slippers or soft soles only. I leave my boots at the front door. I suggest you do the same." There was no doubt it wasn't a suggestion.

Steph placed Brett's mug in front of him and picked hers up.

She backed away to lean against the counter and watched their exchange.

"Thank you, darlin'." Brett smiled warmly and winked with the eye out of Lola's sight. He turned toward his employee. "This is the last time I'm going to tell you this. You and I have nothing together. Not now, or ever. Stay out of my personal life. What goes on between me and Steph is none of your business. One word out of you and you're fired. Do I make myself clear?"

She nodded sullenly. Steph hid her smirk behind her coffee cup.

"From now on, you'll abide by Steph's house rules. That includes no pointy heels and no special room service. In fact, no room service at all, or special meals. You'll eat with the rest of us or go hungry. The staff are not your personal slaves."

"I don't mind setting aside breakfast for her."

"I mind." Brett scowled at Lola and smiled at Steph. He placed his hands on the table and pushed himself up. His forearms bulged deliciously, sending curls of excitement coursing through her traitorous body. Dang, he was sexy. Way too sexy.

"Join me on my walk?" He offered his elbow to her.

"I need to make breakfast."

"I've got breakfast. I am the chef." Penny wandered into the kitchen wearing yesterday's blouse, with JT right behind her.

Steph bit back a teasing comment on her friend's attire and fraternizing with guests. Had her friend finally succumbed to her feelings for JT and slept with him? She hoped so, it was time Penny shed her hang-ups about becoming like her loose-moralled mother. Besides, Penny was cautious and wouldn't do anything to damage the inn's reputation.

"Go. Walk. Take a few hours off."

"I took last night off."

"And you'll take this morning off, too." Penny waved toward the door.

"This is ridiculous." Lola shoved away from the table and stomped toward the door. "The staff doesn't even work."

"Shoes!" Brett barked. When she stepped out of them with a grimace, he spoke again. "I slipped a list of calls I need made under your door. Please make them." Without waiting for a response, he turned toward Steph. "You have no excuse now. Grab a cup and we'll walk."

"Get out of here." Penny laughed. "Be gone and don't come back before breakfast is served."

JT snickered.

"I guess I know when to submit gracefully. Is it okay if I get shoes first?" She waggled a slippered foot.

"Go. Get your shoes. I'll put your coffee in a travel mug." Penny propelled her gently toward the door. In no time at all, before she even wrapped her brain around what was happening, they'd found their boots and were ushered outside.

The morning air was cool. Fred, her Shepherd-Lab cross hurried across the deck, his tail wagging. "Hey, Old Fred." She scratched his ears until he flopped over, exposing his belly for attention. Brett knelt and obliged him with a belly rub.

Penny was pushing her into Brett's arms and now her dog groveled at his feet. Good gravy, even her dog loved him. "Fred, you're a traitor."

"He knows a good thing when he sees it." Brett laughed. "He's been joining me on all my walks. We're just glad you're coming again this morning. Aren't we, old boy?" He patted his leg and Fred jumped obediently to his feet.

They wandered slowly through the yard, past the firepit and down toward the barns. Fluffy white clouds skittered across the sky, dappling the ground with shade. Chickadees called from the trees and squirrels jumped from limb to limb scolding them as they passed. Peace and contentment stole through her, washing away her unpleasant encounter with Lola.

"I have to ask you something," she blurted. "What's up with Lola? She's riding me like I'm fit to steal your fortune or rip you away from your fans. Or her." Oh lord, she hadn't meant to say anything, let alone say it that way.

Brett laughed ruefully. "I honestly don't know. We've been friends. She did save me from a rabid fan once, just once, by pretending to be my girlfriend. This possessiveness is new; but rest assured, she doesn't speak for me."

They walked in silence. The idea of a friendship between Brett and Lola annoyed her, but everyone had a past.

But, where did that leave her? Or leave them? Her attraction to Brett was undeniable and growing stronger by the day. The longer he stayed, the more she gravitated to his side. Honestly, her work was starting to suffer. The day before yesterday she'd resorted to locking herself in the office and had stayed there until she was caught up. If she hadn't, she'd never have been able to afford the time to spend most of the day with Brett yesterday.

Steph and Brett ended up atop a small hill overlooking a cow-mown valley. Her grandfather had fenced in a small area and cemented in a bench where he and his wife spent quiet time every evening, rain or shine, until they retired. They still sat here when they returned to the ranch for a visit. Grampa and Grandma's love was as strong today as the day they married. Steph wanted a love like theirs, one that didn't fade with time or stress.

She sat beside Brett, almost but not touching him. Warmth penetrated her arm and thigh from his closeness. He smelled like heaven. Manly, clean and citrusy, all overlaid with a hint of coffee. She inhaled the precious scent and held it close to her heart before it pooled as arousal low in her belly. They'd shared what? Two? Three? Maybe four kisses. She wanted more. More kisses and more time with him. Time to get to know him better. Yesterday was a glimpse of how well they meshed and had whet her appetite for more.

With him only being here short term and the time being over half gone, anything more than the friendship they'd shared seemed impossible; and she certainly wasn't cut out to live the life he loved. Nor was he going to give up his life for hers.

"You're deep in thought; care to share?" His voice was low and sexy, a caress to her heightened sensations.

"What is this?" She glanced at him from the corner of her eye. He'd think she was nuts.

"What is this what? Do you mean what's happening between us?"

She gave him a 'seriously' look. "Come on, Brett. We're spending mornings and evenings together. Usually alone. We nearly did it at the creek."

"Ah. First, we didn't nearly *do it* at the creek. We nearly made love and we would have, if you hadn't been freezing to death. As for this…" He made air quotes around the word. "I like you. A lot. You seem to like me."

"Is this a friendship, or something more?" She twisted her hands in her lap and tipped her head to stare at the sky. Silence reigned for several agonizing minutes.

"Hell if I know." He shifted on the bench to lean over her. He smiled softly and brushed his lips against hers. "I don't know," he whispered against her lips. "We have such different lifestyles and I don't think either of us is prepared to change them at this point. It leaves us between a rock and a hard place. A real hard place." He waggled his eyebrows. "You're not like anyone I've ever met. You don't care about my fame, or my money. You're not the typical fan."

"I do love your music."

His chuckle was a warm caress. He slung his arm around her and pressed his forehead against hers. "I honestly don't know what's between us. More than friendship, less than a relationship."

"Isn't friendship a relationship?"

"Are you splitting hairs?" He ran a finger down her cheek. Goosebumps rose in its wake. "I'd like to explore this *relationship* and see where it goes. But, I'm not sure how to carry on, so I haven't pressed things. I stopped the casual train years ago."

"You're telling me it's been years since you were with a woman?" She twisted out of his arms to stare at him. "I call shenanigans."

"Yes, I've had relationships with women. What I haven't had is casual sex. I only have protected sex and never with someone I don't care about." Sincerity rippled through his voice and he met her gaze without flinching.

His words echoed in her head. Did that mean he didn't care about her? At all? They'd shared a lot of themselves with each other. It hadn't felt like nothing. She'd fallen for him days ago. She couldn't pinpoint the exact moment; her feelings had come on like a slow breeze stealing into her heart. He'd lodged there now, filling a space she hadn't known was empty.

"What if I said I'd like more? What if I wanted a deeper relationship with you?" *Please, don't let him say no.* Why was she pushing this? It wasn't his fame or his money; he was right. It was him. The way he helped out around the ranch, and the respect he showed his band; respect that was returned. It was the way he stood up for her and made Lola back down. But primarily it was in his love for Elijah and his genuine caring attitude toward everyone. He was a good man.

"Do you want more? What if we can't work out a future? What if things go awry?" His question made her squirm.

She took in his expressionless face, wondering why he kept it so blank. "Nothing in this world comes with a guarantee, especially not relationships. I think we're both mature enough to be honest and to test drive this and see where it goes."

"And my career? You've been through a lot; do you want to risk being in the public eye again?"

She considered his words. The question was logical but premature. "Is there any need for the press to find out? They don't know where you are, there's been nothing in the paper or on the internet since your last concert."

She stood and paced around the bench; cold slithered in where his warm body had rested. Or was it an emotional chill? She couldn't shake the feeling she was risking everything by asking for more. But she was ready to move beyond hand-holding and long sunset walks. She wanted to know him more intimately; in all senses of the word.

She placed her hands on his shoulders and leaned into him. "The truth is, I like you. A lot. I'd like to see where this goes. No promises, no rules, no publicity. Just you and me, seeing where things go. If it doesn't work out, we walk away. No hurt, no complaining."

He smiled up at her, grabbed her hips and pulled her forward until she straddled his lap. "I think..." he brushed a kiss over her lips, "...I can live with that."

His hands burned like hot steel, melting her from the outside in. She covered his fingers with hers and squeezed. His hair tickled her palms as she slid them upwards, tracing the contours of his arms. She smoothed over the folded-up cuffs of his shirt, caressing him through the soft cotton of his western shirt. Rock solid muscles flexed under her hands.

Without warning, a wave of possessiveness washed over her. She cupped his face, tilting it up to hers and devoured his mouth. He tasted like dark roast coffee with sweet undertones of mint and man.

His hands slid up to cup her face. He tilted her right and moved left, trailing kisses of liquid heat down her neck and across her collarbones to pool in her core. A simple touch, and a few kisses and she was gone. Thank the heavens she was kneeling, because if she'd been standing, she'd have fallen. No man's touch had ever affected her like this. She was putty in his hands; warm, willing, pliable. Her heart skittered in her chest. This had to be more than physical attraction. This wasn't about arousal, or sex, this was about this man's, Brett's, effect on her heart.

She nibbled his earlobe, delighting in his soft inhalation of surprise. She kissed down his neck, burying her face in his shoulder, reveling in his heat. She paused, inhaling deeply, memorizing him, storing this moment away for when they were apart. She'd like to believe they could build something together, but doubts lingered and she'd need moments like this to get her through when he moved on. She pushed the uncertainty away, she wouldn't let fear steal her joy.

She moved lower, following the opening of his shirt until his buttons halted her progress. She wiggled her fingers between them and fumbled to slip the tiny disc through the opening. His breath hissed out, making her smile.

CHAPTER 9

⧖

Her lips felt like heaven on his throat. Damn. He'd gone from content to confused and now to fully aroused and hard as steel in three minutes. His head was reeling, either from her kisses or the abrupt change of emotions.

He'd been battling his attraction all week, it was a relief to have a direction for their relationship. He hadn't come here looking for anything more than a rest before performing at Stampede, but she'd managed to turn his world upside down without doing anything but be herself. She was one hell of a woman. Kind, compassionate, strong, defiant, funny and playful. He'd enjoyed every minute he'd spent with her. Guilt niggled at his mind. He'd gone after her, hard, when he'd learned she was Elijah's teacher. How wrong he'd been! He didn't know how he'd ever make up for his screw-up, although she seemed to have moved past it.

God, her hands and lips felt glorious against his skin. Each nibble and lick sent blood rushing from his brain to his groin. If she kept this up, he'd never be able to walk to the house. Her fingers tangled with his shirt as he stroked her shoulders and arms. Damn!

He cupped her hands in his and held them still. "Hey. Hey."

"Mm?" She kept kissing, stealing his train of thought.

"We need to stop this," he muttered, forcing the words from his dry mouth. They couldn't do this here, in the middle of a field in public. Anyone could come by. He wouldn't do that to her. He wouldn't shame her by risking getting caught. Their passion could wait for a more private venue.

"I thought—" She leaned back, the color drained from her face and she looked angry or maybe upset. Women confused him. He could write a damned good love song, adored by millions of women, but he sure as hell didn't understand them.

"I want you. You have no idea how much." He thrust his hips up gently, pressing his erection against her core. He smiled and stroked her cheek. "I want you; I need you. But we can't do this here. I won't take you like an animal. You deserve better. Privacy, a soft bed."

"What if I want it here? Now?" She ground against him. "It might be fun outdoors."

"Hell, yes. But not now, not this close to the house, anyone could come by and see us. Is five minutes of pleasure worth weeks or months of embarrassment?"

"Five minutes. You're only good for five minutes? Maybe I need to rethink this." Her grin told him she was teasing. She sighed and dropped her head to his shoulder, hiding her face and mumbled something incoherent against his neck.

He nipped her ear and soothed it with his tongue. "Funny. Very funny. You'll regret that." He started tickling her, not stopping until she begged for mercy. "Never doubt my prowess." He winked.

She studied him, pursing her lips. "I expect you to prove me wrong. Or I'll announce it to the whole world that Brett Wyatt's real name is Quick Draw." She giggled and bolted off his lap. She ran hell bent for leather down the hill away from the house.

Laughing, he chased after her, shouting out warnings. He let her run for a minute and put on a burst of speed, caught her around the waist and spun her in a circle. Gently, he set her on her feet, then turned her to face him. "I'll see you tonight. Your room. After everyone has gone to bed."

"Indeed?" She smirked and raised one eyebrow.

"Indeed." He agreed before taking her mouth with his. Several minutes later, breathless from the short run and their kiss, they walked to the house hand in hand. A small smile played on her lips. He was tempted to ask what she was thinking, but he suspected her thoughts were probably in line with his.

There was a lot to look forward to with this enticing dynamic woman. She called to him, and his body answered. He hoped to hell the condom in his wallet wasn't expired.

"Do you ever go to Stampede?"

She paused to look at him. "I used to go every year; but not recently. Why?"

"Just wondering. I'm playing there next week, I've got three shows. I thought you might like to come to one. I know a guy in the band." He winked. "I can get you a backstage pass."

"I'd love to see you perform, again. I saw you the last time you performed in Calgary. You're a fabulous stage artist. You really know how to work the crowd."

It didn't take a rocket scientist to hear the unspoken concern in her voice. "I've got three shows. You can take your pick. Come to as many as you want."

"I don't think so but thank you." She slid her arm around his waist and leaned into him.

"Do the crowds worry you? It's not like we'll tour the barns or ride the Ferris wheel. We go in by private van and out the same way. Nobody will see you."

"I don't know— Since the accident, I haven't been in a crowd in a long time. I barely leave the ranch. But man, I do love cotton candy and those little donuts. I used to tour the barns and check out the livestock, too. Not that I know more than just the basics about cattle or horses."

The vulnerability in her voice was a kick in the conscience. Was it really so difficult for her to risk being recognized? Two years had passed since the media circus. He'd never been subject to negative press, just positive praise and the occasional rumor or innuendo about his dating and sex life; but he recognized the pain the past must have caused her.

"I won't press you; but I expect the media is onto bigger and better things now. Think about it?" God, he hated the pleading in his voice. He wanted her to accompany him to the shows but his voice stank of desperation. Why was it so important to have her at a performance?

"I've seen you perform. Last time you were in Calgary. Floor seats. Fifth row, dead center. It was up close and personal and the first time you sang Laughing Heart in concert. You're an incredible performer. You feed off the fans' energy. The more they're into it, the more you seem to get back. I nearly cried when you sang with the little girl in the wheelchair."

"Francine. She was so sweet. Her heart surgery went well. She's up and around now and able to function without the chair most of the time."

"How did you find her?"

"Her grandmother wrote to me. She was terrified Francine wouldn't survive the surgery and wanted to give her a special gift. Something happy and positive to carry her through. I'm not sure I had anything to do with her making it, I credit the outstanding heart surgeons at the Stollery Children's Hospital in Edmonton for her recovery. I was glad to offer her a bit of happiness."

"You have a special guest at most of your concerts, don't you?"

"Word gets around. I don't reply to trivial requests, but life and death situations and last wishes, yeah, I respond to those. Kids are precious and if I can make their last days, or their illness better, I'll do it. I visit the Alberta Children's Hospital in Calgary as well as the Stollery whenever I'm nearby."

She shoulder-bumped him. "That's an understatement. You

visit all of Canada's children's hospitals." She chuckled and smiled up at him. "You're a good man, Brett Wyatt."

"I don't know about that, but kids are special people." She leaned into him, her short frame fit perfectly against his tall one; like she was made for him. They seemed to mesh, physically and emotionally. He'd miss her when he was gone; unless they found a way to spend time together while he toured.

God, he was thinking like a hormone-crazed teenager. He couldn't deny he wanted her, more than he'd wanted any woman in a long time, maybe ever, but he wasn't a lovesick fool. Was he?

On the porch, out of sight of the windows, he turned and kissed her. Her arms slipped around his waist, pulling him closer, revealing her need. "Think about it. Please." He brushed his lips against hers, they separated, entered the house and returned to the real world. Breakfast, and his band members awaited.

∼

STEPH PACED AROUND HER SUITE. From the door, through her private sitting room, into the bedroom and out again. Back and forth. Back and forth. Brett had gone to his room three hours ago. It was pushing one in the morning. If he didn't show up soon, she'd have to go to bed. She couldn't stay up all night. She had an inn to run.

Insecurity plagued her and ugly thoughts ran through her mind. What if he'd changed his mind? What if he hadn't been serious when he whispered his plan to come to her room tonight? Self-doubt plagued her. She never should have considered fraternizing with a guest, let alone a famous one. He was probably with his band, laughing at her naivety. She wrapped her arms around herself and paused in front of the roaring fireplace, hoping to expel the chill of regret and self-doubt.

It was time to give up on him. She removed the wine from the ice bucket and stowed the glasses in her small bar. Time to shed the sexy black and red silk lingerie set she'd bought on a whim last year. She turned toward the bedroom when a light knock sounded on her door. She hurried over.

"Yes?" she asked quietly through the door.

"It's Brett," he whispered. "Open the door before someone sees me."

She flipped the lock and he slipped through the door, easing it shut behind him. "God, I thought I'd never get here." He wrapped his arms around her, urged her against the wall and brushed his lips across hers.

Relief and arousal flooded through her. "You almost missed me. I was headed to bed."

He leaned back, his gaze took her in from head to toe, pausing leisurely several times in each direction. He studied her sexy satin chemise, it revealed as much as it covered up and the effect was breathtaking.

"Hot damn. You look incredible." He nuzzled her neck. "And you smell divine. Thank God I finally made it here. I ran into Lola, then Tucker. Do you have any idea how hard it is to fake exhaustion, when I needed desperately to be rid of them, so I could come to you?"

She laughed. "Poor baby." She teased him to cover up her fear that he might have changed his mind; he could still back out. She was in this, full bore, no regrets, but she still had doubts. She studied his eyes, searching for clues to his feelings. Was this just sex for him? She'd spent the entire day trying to figure out where she stood. Her emotions were in turmoil; running the gamut from teenaged enthusiasm to blinding fear and insecurity.

She wanted him, not just physically. She was hooked on him; she needed him and she'd decided to take what he was offering and let the future sort itself out. Maybe they had something, maybe they didn't. Only time would tell and tonight she'd take everything he offered.

"I see you came fully clothed."

"I could hardly wander the halls half-naked, could I?"

He traced the lace edge of her nightgown, down the left side between her breasts and up the right. Shivers followed and goosebumps prickled in the wake of his feather-light caress. He nibbled her ear, she tipped her head left and breathed out a sigh. "Oh."

"Mm. Like that?" His breath was hot against her skin.

"I think you're wearing entirely too many clothes." She fumbled with his buttons. After struggling with the first one, she quickly released the rest and tugged his shirt from his jeans. Grabbing him by the belt, she guided him through the sitting room and into her bedroom.

He halted at the foot of the bed. "Are you sure?"

His words, his soft, cautious tone removed any lingering doubts.

"I've never been so sure of anything in my life. I want you, Brett Wyatt. Right here, right now."

She backed up, pulling him with her, until her legs bumped the end of the mattress. Wrapping her arms around his shoulders, she pressed her lips to his and fell backward, drawing him down on top of her. He braced himself with his hands, landing gently, without crushing her.

She lifted her head and nibbled his chin. He was smooth as glass, he must have shaved after dinner. Fabulous. Now there was no fear of tell-tale whisker burns causing raised eyebrows in the morning. She smiled up at him. This was exactly where she wanted to be; cozy, hot and ready. But, more importantly, in his arms. She wiggled her legs free and wrapped them around his waist. "Come here. Kiss me." He lowered himself closer and their lips met.

∼

"Before we head downstairs this morning, I want to know if you've considered my request." Brett tugged at a lock of Steph's hair.

Dread churned in her stomach. She smiled at him, hiding her nerves. She rolled toward him and snuggled into the curve of his shoulder, hiding her face.

"I know you hate being in public."

Her chest tightened.

"But, I want you to come to a performance. I've got three this week. It's a lot to ask, but I'm asking. Just one show. Please."

She tensed under him, resisting the urge to bolt and end the conversation. He was asking a lot, probably more than she could handle. She wanted to say yes. She needed to say no. He wouldn't have asked if it wasn't important to him. All new relationships took give and take. Could she give him this? She chewed her lip indecisively.

"Honey, I see you're nervous and I understand why. We'll keep you backstage. Nobody will see you."

Crap on toast. She would have to say yes. Where would she find the courage? What if the press noticed her? Could she face her worst fear? This scared her more than spiders. Maybe she could get some anti-anxiety drugs. If she was doped up she'd be able to handle it. *Right.* She hated taking over-the-counter drugs. She certainly wasn't about to take prescription drugs on a lark.

"You know I can see every thought pass over your face? Right?" He stroked one finger down her cheek. "I'd like to perform for you. I'd like you to see what I see when I'm on stage. But, I understand if you're not able to go."

She looked up at him. Hope, patience and caring mingled in his eyes. She might have an expressive face, but his eyes told her how important this was. Then, it dawned on her.

His family.

They'd never watched him perform and they didn't like his career choice even though he was successful. He needed her approval.

"I'll come." She paused. "If you can find a way to keep me out of the crowd and away from the media."

His smile was like the sun bursting out from behind the clouds, making her entire day brighter.

"I'll find a way. It won't be hard. You can travel with the band. We take a van right up to the venue. I promise you, you won't regret this. Thank you." His arms snaked around her waist, their heat chasing away the chill that settled in her chest.

CHAPTER 10

Steph stood with Tucker in the wings of the Saddledome stage after Brett's performance. The man was magnificent. He sang, danced and wooed the crowd for nearly two hours. Now, he was giving his third, and hopefully final encore song. She couldn't wait to get out of here. She'd relaxed and enjoyed a concert she'd dreamed of attending. Now, with things wrapping up, doubts of escaping unnoticed wracked her nerves.

"Aren't you worried about being recognized?" She leaned in close so Tucker could hear her over the roaring crowd.

"Not really, no. It used to bother me. Now, I've made it my campaign to remind people to be conscious of their surroundings and of what might go wrong. The media has started ignoring me because they don't get the outraged reaction I used to give. There's peace in knowing Elijah's death might open some eyes to potential dangers." He shrugged. "Relax, Steph. It'll pass and you'll be fine. Trust the universe to make things better for you."

"I'll try." Her words lacked conviction, but it was the best she had.

"I'm off for a drink with friends," Tucker informed them. "I won't be back to the inn tonight. You and Brett should take in the nightlife. You've got an hour or more until things start shutting down. Take in a few rides, play some games. Visit the beer gardens."

"With a celebrity? Are you nuts?"

"Come on, Steph." Brett's voice came from behind her. He slipped his arm around her shoulder. "I'll go incognito. It'll be fun."

His wink sent heat flooding through her. Could she do this?

"I don't know…"

"Come on, I'll change clothes, put on a ball cap and fake glasses. Nobody will even notice. You'll love it."

"What the heck." She clapped her hands excitedly. "I haven't been to Stampede since I moved to Toronto. I miss the hustle and bustle and I'll kill for a corn dog."

"Yuck." Tucker laughed. "I'm out of here. I'll catch up with you guys tomorrow."

"Come one, I'll get changed and we'll hit the Stampede grounds. How do you feel about heights?"

"Uneasy." She chuckled. "But, if we go unnoticed, I'll try anything once."

Brett slipped out of his show boots and into sneakers. He traded the swirled blue shirt they'd bought on their shopping trip for a T-shirt and denim jacket. With fake Clark Kent glasses and a ball cap, she barely recognized him.

"Wow. If I hadn't seen it, your transformation, I wouldn't believe it."

They slipped out the door and were lost in the crowd in minutes.

Steph grabbed Brett's arm. "Do you smell that?" She didn't wait for an answer, she yanked on his hand and pulled him through the crowd. "Let's grab some food and check out the displays in the BMO Centre."

"What about the rides?"

"Maybe later. My girlfriend has a quilt in the show. I want to see if she won a prize." After a short wait for mini-donuts and sodas they wandered into the exhibition hall. Steph hurried along, oblivious to the throng of people walking past them.

"Whoa, wait." Brett called. "Look at this."

Steph paused.

Crap.

He stood in front of an enormous display of Stampede Royalty pictures. She'd hurried past it hoping to distract him.

"Is that you?" Surprise and disbelief filled his voice. His stare pivoted between her and the picture.

She flushed from her collar to her hairline. "Yeah."

"That's quite the hairdo. You never told me you were a Stampede Princess."

"I would have—eventually. And big hair was popular then."

"You were as beautiful then as you are now. How old were you?"

"Twenty-one. I tried three times before I made it into the finals. When I made Princess, I decided that was good enough."

"They let you compete more than once? Is that normal?"

She shrugged. "Okay, I tried some smaller rodeos and fairs. Then, when I hit university, I went out for the big one. It opened a lot of doors for me. I met some wonderful contacts who I still interact with. It was great fun, but a lot of work." She chuckled as they walked on.

"By the end of Stampede, I swore I'd never eat another pancake or serve another sausage. We attend at least two breakfasts every day. Dinners, store openings, concerts, rodeos. Television, newspapers. The list was endless. It was fabulous fun, but so exhausting."

"I didn't realize I was dating a celebrity." He tugged a lock of her hair.

"You're wrong, you're the celebrity."

He clamped a hand over her mouth and looked furtively

around the exhibition. "Shh, don't give me away. I could use a night out without fans." His voice rocked with laughter.

They finished their snack and wandered deeper into the displays. "Oh, there it is." She pointed to a navy, cream and gold quilt hanging high overhead. "Amanda's quilt. Look, look." She wiggled on her toes. "She won a prize. I can't see what it is. Can you see?"

"I can't read it, but it's blue. Is blue good?"

"Blue is amazing! I can't believe she won." She flung her arms around his neck and kissed his cheek.

A flash of light exploded in her face.

"Whoa!" They separated and turned toward the light.

"You're Brett Wyatt." A twenty-something blonde woman pointed her cell phone at them and snapped another picture. "Can I get an autograph?"

"Sorry, miss. You're mistaken," Brett said in a fake German accent.

"I'd know you anywhere. I just left your concert. I can't believe you're walking around like a regular person. Please, please, please, can I have your autograph?"

Heads were starting to turn their way. Steph's stomach clenched. This was going to be a disaster. People started whispering and pointing.

"If I give you an autograph will you leave us alone and forget you saw us?"

"Yes, oh gosh, yes." She rummaged in her purse and handed him a paper and pen.

"What's your name?" He kept up the accent, Steph nearly laughed.

"Melissa. Make it out to Melissa." She giggled excitedly. "My friends will never believe this."

He signed with a flourish and handed the paper back. She grinned and read it. "Pleased to meet you, Melissa. Wait? Heinrich Schmidt. Who's Heinrich Schmidt?"

"I am, and this is my wife, Elsa." Steph nodded.

"Um... err." The girl stammered. "I thought—"

"Sorry to disappoint you. We come from Germany with our friends, every year, for Stampede. Something about the Western way of life keeps bringing us back. Sorry to disappoint you."

Melissa blushed to the roots of her hair. "Sorry to bother you." She turned and shuffled away.

Holding in their laughter, Steph and Brett bolted for the exit.

"Oh gosh. I can't believe you did that!" Steph leaned against the building's wall and gasped for breath. "That was the worst accent I have ever heard, and she bought it." She stopped laughing. "Do you trick fans often?"

"That's the first time I've ever denied a fan. I've used the disguise before; but if I'm ever recognized, I just go with the flow and sign autographs. Tonight, I didn't; because you wanted anonymity. Your privacy is important to me."

Gratitude rushed through her. "You didn't have to; but thank you." She brushed a kiss across his cheek.

∼

Two nights later, Steph stood just behind the curtain of the Coca-Cola Stage, inside the main Stampede ground gates. The return trip to the Stampede grounds had been uneventful as Brett promised. Nobody paid any attention to her as she exited the van with the band. The pressure in her chest wasn't as bad as the first concert, but it was still there. It eased as she realized she was safe from the crowd and the few milling reporters and cameramen.

The stage was an enormous outdoor venue and the Stampede hosted several concerts every day, all free with admission.

"I love that these concerts are free to the audience. Not everyone can afford regular concert ticket prices." Brett grinned at her. "I like to give back where I can. A free concert does that."

This was his last concert. In two days, he'd be headed home.

She dreaded his departure. Part of her knew he'd call. The rest of her was certain tonight was the end of their relationship.

The crowd mingled noisily, excitement filling the air. A roar of applause rent the air as the band strolled on stage. A quick tune-up of instruments and they launched into their traditional opening song, a fast-paced number about drinking beer and weekends. Twenty seconds of music passed before Brett joined them on stage and the crowd went wild. Women screamed and called his name. Wolf whistles and shouts of approval settled in as he stopped, center stage, and tipped his hat. The band paused.

"Evening all. How's everyone doing tonight?" The crowd roared. "All right then, let's get this party started." The band resumed playing the weekend-beer song with the crowd singing along.

Steph stood watching Brett from backstage. He danced and sang and wooed the ladies. He teased, ribbed and needled the men. The concert was divine. She'd noticed last night that he'd really honed his skills in the past two years; Brett Wyatt was one hell of an entertainer. They performed a dozen songs and the band paused again.

"Tonight, I'd like to introduce a special guest. Come on out here, Tommy. Everyone, give a big hand for Tommy." The crowd obliged as a security guard escorted a young, red-headed woman and her son onto the stage to stand nervously beside Brett.

"I'm gonna tell y'all a story. Tommy here has a rare form of leukemia." The crowd quieted. "His daddy passed away last year, and his poor mama is havin' trouble makin' ends meet. Now, y'all know my charity helps out sick kids and folks in need. Special folks like Tommy and his mama; but I'm asking you to dig deep into your pockets and give them a little help, so his mama can take time away from work to accompany him to his treatments."

Ten tall, lean men in navy and white western shirts with white Stetsons stepped onto the stage. "These gentlemen are gonna pass through the crowd collecting donations while we finish the set. Dig deep folks, help little Tommy out."

Tommy and his mother hugged Brett and thanked him and the band as the cowboys descended the stairs to work the crowd. Steph peeked through the curtains, men pulled out their wallets and women dug in their purses and handed over their hard-earned money to help Tommy. Tears welled in Steph's eyes.

God bless Brett Wyatt and his enormous heart. She watched him chat to the crowd for a moment, making merry as if he'd done nothing special. Her breathing grew tight and happiness flowed through her. Her hand flew to her mouth to hide her smile.

Sweet heaven, she loved him. She wrapped her arms around herself in a hug, savoring the feeling, reveling in the emotional moment. It wasn't often one fell in love, and it was even more rare that you knew the exact moment. She'd treasure this moment, this concert and this man for the rest of her life.

The drummer tapped out a beat and the band launched into another song. Halfway through, Brett's voice wobbled, just slightly. She doubted the ecstatic crowd noticed, but the drummer and bass guitar player exchanged glances. Tucker swore under his breath. This couldn't be good. He'd mentioned voice trouble, but she thought he meant he was overtired. The past three weeks of rest should have cured his voice, shouldn't it? Two songs later, the final song of the night, his voice cracked. Hard. He finished the song and bowed.

"Guess that's all, folks." He cleared his throat. "Seems my cold's caught up with me. Y'all have a great evening and enjoy Stampede." He bowed again and sauntered off the stage.

"Come on, Steph. Time to go." He grabbed her hand and urged her along. "The band will catch up later. We'll take the van home."

She hurried along, and glanced over her shoulder at the band. They huddled together, just off stage talking frantically. She wished she was closer; something was up and she'd bet her life it was related to the distortions in his voice.

In no time at all he had her bundled into the van, with a Stampede staff member driving them off the grounds. This late in the evening, the crowd was starting to thin and it took only moments to reach the exit gate. The driver, a twenty-something cowboy, parked and turned toward the back seat. "Great concert, man. Love your music. Would it be incredibly rude to ask for an autograph?"

Brett laughed woodenly and reached for the concert T-shirt and black marker the driver held out to him. "No problem." He signed with a flourish and handed the shirt and marker back. "We've got it from here. Thanks for getting us off the grounds in one piece."

Grinning like he'd just won the lottery, the driver loped away, leaving Brett and Steph sitting in the backseat of the band's van.

"Now what?"

"Now, you drive us home."

"Me?" she squeaked. "Don't you want to drive?" Men always wanted to drive.

"I'm beyond tired. I'd appreciate it if you took the wheel." He looked at her, his expression somewhere between expectation and pleading.

"Sure. I don't mind." They climbed into the front. Steph in the driver's seat and Brett riding shotgun. A right turn, then a left and she had them speeding south on Macleod Trail toward Okotoks.

Despite her worry, she focused on the road, sparing Brett only an occasional look. An initial glance at Brett indicated he was asleep; his head rested against the seat, his eyes were closed. Another glance, several miles later, revealed his fingers tapping to an unheard, agitated rhythm.

"Want to talk about it?" She spoke low, she didn't want to startle him or increase his agitation. No response. "The concert was lovely. I'm glad you talked me into joining you. Nobody bothered me backstage and the gesture you made for Tommy was so kind. How much money does something like that bring in?"

"Not enough to make a difference. I'll top it up before we send her the check."

"Wow. Very nice."

"It's bugger all. I've got more money than I'll ever spend. It costs me nothing." Anger and bitterness dripped from his words and he didn't open his eyes. His fingers tapped faster.

"I beg to differ. The crowd was happy to donate. I watched them. You gave their hearts a lift by showing them someone less fortunate and letting them help out a family in need. Tommy and his mom will be together for his treatments, and all because of you. It's not about how much money you donate, you care enough to try and help. You've got a big heart. You, Brett Wyatt, are a generous man and a good soul."

He grunted and turned his head toward the window.

She kept silent until they reached the outskirts of the city. She kept her eyes on the road. Late evening was a bad time for animals crossing the highway, and she didn't want to happen upon any unexpectedly.

"Half an hour and we'll be home." She peeked over at him.

He'd never said how serious his voice issues were, so she'd done some research on vocal cord injuries. Some were minor and repaired themselves with rest. Others required surgery and could be devastating if left untreated. Either Brett hadn't rested long enough or his damage was more severe than he'd let on. He must be half-petrified with fear of losing his career. She couldn't leave him fester in his fear. She took a deep breath and braced herself for the words she was about to utter.

"I know you're not asleep and you probably want to be left alone. I won't do that. Over the three weeks since you came to the ranch, we've become friends, and more. Friends share their problems. I suspect this has something to do with the inconsistencies in your singing tonight. Your vocal cords aren't healing themselves. You need to see a doctor or risk losing your career."

"Let it go." His hands clenched into fists on his bunched-up thighs.

"I can't, you're my friend. Let me take you to the doctor and get this checked out. Perhaps it's something simple and easily fixed." She pitched her words to be comforting and non-confrontational, but doubted he heard them that way.

"Not now, Steph."

"You told me you'd seen one doctor and he said you needed to rest your voice. Well, you did, for three weeks. In all that time, you only sang on the first night, and lowly at that. I didn't hear any strain then. It's time to take the next step and see a specialist."

"I saw a goddamned specialist. I have vocal cord lesions. They should have healed themselves. My career is over. My life is over."

Wow! Dramatic much? She kept the thoughts to herself. He was upset enough already without her exacerbating the problem. "You can still play, and eventually sing. You just need a break. You love helping kids, maybe you could teach music."

"Yeah, I'm sure my fans would love that. Give it a rest. I don't want to talk about it. Not with you, not with a doctor."

There was a quiver in his voice. Not from the lesions, but from emotion. He sounded on the verge of tears. God, her heart was breaking for him. How bad must this be hurting him? He must be devastated.

She reached out and patted his hand. She held it lightly until his fist unclenched. She slid her fingers under his so their palms touched. "I can't even pretend to know what you're going through; but I do know pain is better shared. I won't press, but I'm here for you. We can talk, or just be together."

He squeezed her hand until she thought he'd crush it. She squeezed back and drove the rest of the way home one-handed. Thank heaven the van was an automatic, unlike her ranch truck with its standard transmission. She parked near the front door and they went inside.

"Good night." He walked to the stairs.

"I'll be right up with tea. I'll douse it in honey and lemon, it'll be soothing."

"Make it bourbon."

He would mention the one booze she didn't have in the house. Since he didn't want tea, she'd find him something suitable, just not what he asked for. She didn't normally serve alcohol to guests, but she'd make an exception this time.

She loaded a tray with ice, two glasses and the best booze she had in the house. Glenmorangie Scotch, Tullamore Dew Irish Whiskey, Grey Goose Vodka, Forty Creek Whisky, an unopened bottle of Patrón Tequila and a bottle of Apothic Inferno red wine. She had no intention of letting him drink it all, she just wanted him to have an option. She threw on a tub of chip dip and stuck a bag of ripple chips in her teeth and struggled her way upstairs.

Hands full, she tapped on his door with her foot.

"It's open." He growled.

"Hands full," she mumbled around the chip bag. He whipped the door open and took the tray and turned his back on her. The room was dim, the yard light outside filtered in through the lacy curtains; the only other illumination came from behind the half-closed bathroom door.

Her mouth dropped open and the chips hit the floor. Holy Hanna. He'd shed his western duds in favor of low-slung silk pajama bottoms and a skin-tight T-shirt. The muscles of his back, shoulders and arms flexed as he crossed the room. Those sexy pajamas threatened to drop with every step. Heat pooled in her belly and flooded her body. Her face went pink and her heart pounded out a staccato beat that had nothing to do with climbing the stairs. How in the world was she going to comfort him without succumbing to desire?

"You gonna pick up those chips or just stare at my ass all day," he asked over his shoulder, his voice hoarse.

"Uh. Er. I haven't decided yet. Hold still and let me consider the options." What else could she say? No sense denying the obvious and it wasn't the first time she'd ogled his butt. He'd caught her more than once since they'd made love last week. At least he'd managed to wrangle half a smile for her.

"I assume you're staying? What'll it be?"

She closed the door, eliminating the hall light and walked up to the dresser where he stood pouring himself a generous serving of Tullamore Dew. He glanced at her, one eyebrow raised. His cocky expression didn't hide the pain in his eyes or the tension in his shoulders.

"Yes, I'm staying; unless you tell me to leave. I'll have the wine, please." She decided to stick to wine because she wasn't much of a drinker and strong spirits went right to her head. She half expected him to kick her out so he could be alone in his misery, but he opened the wine and poured.

They sat together on the small loveseat adjacent to the bed. She leaned into the corner and tucked her feet beneath her, her body turned so she faced him. He stared straight ahead without acknowledging her. She barely touched her wine and he demolished two tumblers of whiskey. This could be a long night.

"Want to talk about it?" she asked at last.

"No."

She banked her irritation. She'd been in his shoes. Nothing anyone said or did brought comfort when you knew your career was over. The only difference was, hers had been shot to hell forever and with treatment, his could continue.

"I've read about this." She fired the opening shot.

"Me, too. That's what worries me." His knuckles turned white on the heavy crystal glass.

"There are treatment options. If rest doesn't work, there's retraining, and in the worst cases, surgical solutions. The chances of success are very high."

He set his glass on the table and flopped onto the loveseat, raking his fingers through his hair, his eyes scrunched shut. "But there's a chance of failure."

Silence fell between them and neither spoke for several minutes. "I think you're looking at this wrong." She was taking a risk pointing out the obvious. "There's a good chance this is temporary and you're focusing on the slim chance of failure. Aren't half your songs about overcoming failure in love and life? Where'd your optimism go?"

"Right down the crapper like my career." The cold bitterness in his voice chilled her to the bone. She wrapped her arms around her waist and persisted in trying to reason with him.

"Your career is by no means over. You haven't even seen a doctor. So, you have to cancel some concerts and really rest this time. Maybe you need surgery. What of it? Your life isn't over. I've heard of musicians who've gotten past vocal cord lesions. If they can continue their career, you can too." She leaned forward and grasped his forearm. "You're a strong man, Brett, you can get through this. I'll help you."

He picked up his glass and slammed the whiskey back. "I think I need to be alone."

"Are you sure?" He was kicking her out? So much for their burgeoning relationship. He didn't speak so she gave his arm a little shake. "Brett."

"Just go. Please." The naked pain and pleading in his voice sliced her heart to ribbons. How could she leave him alone in mental anguish? But, how could she deny his request?

She stood and placed her wine on the tray. Leaving the chips and dip behind with the whiskey and ice, she picked up the tray and with considerable mental effort, left the room and set the tray on a table in the hallway.

"You know where to find me when you need me. I'll be waiting." She eased the door shut behind her. She leaned her forehead against the wall outside his door. She hated to leave him alone like this. Experience had shown her talking a problem through could lessen the burden and perhaps offer alternate solutions. But, in the early stages of a relationship, where they were now, you really couldn't force your partner to talk.

Partner. Ha. Just the thought brought a rueful laugh. They weren't partners; they were friends with benefits. Admittedly the benefits were great. That didn't mean she didn't want their relationship to develop. At this moment, what she wanted, more than anything, was to be inside his room offering comfort and support. If only he'd let her help.

Heart heavy, she returned the alcohol to the liquor cabinet in her private office and sitting room and plodded upstairs to pace her room in private. There was no way she was sleeping; not when he needed her.

Two o'clock rolled around, then three. It was approaching four when she gave in and went to bed. Obviously, he wasn't going to come see her and she needed at least a bit of sleep before facing the band and her duties in the morning.

Six came way too early. She trudged, gritty eyed and weak with exhaustion into the bathroom for a shower. She slapped her damp hair into a sloppy ponytail and made her way to the kitchen with a heavy heart. The only way she'd survive the day was with gallons of coffee and maybe a double shot of Baileys.

She took the long way downstairs, past Brett's room. The door was ajar. Good, he was up and around already. She knocked lightly and entered. The bed hadn't been slept in; he must have stayed up all night. Something was amiss; she looked around trying to figure out what was making her uneasy.

Why had he left the door open? He wasn't here. She called his name softly, not wanting to disturb the other guests. No answer. It hit her like a bullet to the chest. He'd left. There wasn't a single personal item left in the room. Not one! She checked the bathroom; no shaving kit, no shampoo, no comb. He'd taken everything and run like a thief in the night. Without even saying goodbye.

She leaned against the bathroom doorjamb, tears streaming

down her cheeks. He'd been scared last night, now he was scared and alone. He could have told her he was going. Didn't he owe her at least that much?

She wiped her eyes and blew her nose and took a moment to wash her face with cool water. No sense letting everyone else know he'd dumped her without a word. She pulled the room's door shut behind her and hurried to the kitchen. Maybe she'd catch him before he left.

CHAPTER 11

He was a coward. A good-for-nothing, yellow-bellied coward.

Brett huddled in his seat on the private jet he'd hired to take him home, berating himself for running without saying goodbye. Steph wasn't a casual kind of girl; he'd known commitment was important from the start. After spending so much time with her, he was doubly sure. What they shared was serious and had the potential to turn long-term, if they could reconcile their careers. And, he'd cut and run like a chicken shit.

Tucker had shown up at Brett's room late last night; he'd called in some favors and gotten Brett an appointment for late today with Toronto's premier ENT specialist. How he'd managed that in the middle of the night was a mystery. Fame had its perks. The doctor was a huge Brett Wyatt fan and eager to help out.

There'd been more than enough time to say goodbye, but he couldn't face Steph. Like a coward, he'd coerced Tucker into flying home with him. They climbed into his truck and headed for the airport. He hired a private charter company to take him home. He left his truck in their parking lot. The rental company would pick it up there. Guilt ate away at his guts like acid through concrete. He should have said goodbye, but he'd chickened out. If his voice was gone, he was nothing and he wouldn't stick around and drag Steph down with him.

Bullshit. Even he didn't believe his silent lies.

He was in full flight mode and had panicked. He had no idea how to deal with this and didn't want to worry about a relationship at the same time. He'd made off like a thief in the night; fully aware his actions would kill their relationship. She deserved better than a coward with a soon-to-be failed, career.

His parents would be tickled. They'd love it if he left the public eye and assumed a normal career like his brothers. He chided himself silently. They'd love to see him join the real world, but for all their faults, his family wouldn't want him to lose his passion. He winced. His mother wouldn't want him treating a woman badly either.

Heartburn bubbled in his guts, searing his esophagus. He should have bought antacids. He'd used them a lot in the early days when he was struggling to make ends meet but had outgrown needing them as his fame had increased. He'd better have some at home; acid reflux could exacerbate his issues.

At five that afternoon, he paced the ENT's tiny exam room waiting for the report on the scope the doc had performed.

"Brett, I've got the results." The doctor stepped inside and closed the door behind him. "You don't just have damaged vocal cords, they're full of scar tissue from continually using them when you should have been resting. I've examined your tour schedule. You don't take enough time during your tour to rest."

"Nobody does. Not me, or any other singer." He objected, refusing to accept blame for what was clearly his fault. "Why doesn't this happen to other artists?"

"Nobody knows. It's not an easy thing to research. Some singers can perform every night and not get damage. You, on the other hand, should have rested more. I'd suggest time off and no singing, but it's too late for that. The only option, besides giving up your career, is to surgically remove the scar tissue."

Brett winced. He needed to put his voice on the line by risking surgery? He sucked in a breath. It took conscious effort to shake off his frustration and speak rationally.

"What if I took a couple years off? I'm not comfortable going under the knife." Frankly, it scared him to death. Calm on the outside, his insides quivered with fear.

"Can you go an entire year, or two, without singing at all, without shouting or raising your voice? I doubt it. Even then, chances are your issue will persist and you'll still need surgery. My recommendation is to get on this right away. I've checked my schedule. We can reserve a space for you tomorrow, as there's been a cancellation in day surgery. Protocol dictates surgeries cancelled with less than twenty-four hours' notice are not rebooked, leaving the space available for emergencies. I can give you the spot. An hour under sedation, some laser cutting and you'll be on your way to a concert before you know it."

"I don't know—"

"I'm going to give it to you straight. There are risks. Complications are rare, but your damage is severe, the worst I've ever seen in twenty-five years of doing this. There's a chance of permanent damage, the risk is low, less than five percent, but there is a risk. And, as it is with all anesthetic procedures, there's a slight possibility of complications. Have you ever been under anesthetic?"

"Never, just some freezing at the dentist." He paused, his thoughts ricocheting around his brain. *Could he risk this?* Could he put his career on the line on the off chance surgery would heal him?

"Before you decide, you need to know that if you don't get this done, your career is probably over. If we go ahead, you'll be in the hospital for a minimum of one night, maybe two. When you go home, there'll be strict instructions on follow-up care. No singing. None. No singing for at least three months; maybe more depending on the severity of the scarring. I'll give you ten minutes to think it over." He paused with his hand on the door. "Think fast, my friend. It'd be a shame if the world lost your music."

"Uh. Yeah."

The small room squeezed in on him, stealing his breath, fueling his panic. How in the hell was he supposed to make a decision like this in ten minutes? It affected his entire life, especially his career. Dammit, he should have brought Steph home with him. He needed someone to talk this over with.

Well, that horse had bolted. He was stuck now, thanks to his own stupidity, and had to make the decision alone. He cussed a blue streak, his voice barely more than a whisper. He doubted there was anyone left in the office except the doctor, but if there was, he didn't want to disturb them. Neither did he want to scream and risk further damage. He slammed his hands on the exam table over and over, shredding the thin paper covering. He scrunched the shreds into a ball and ripped them apart before stuffing the wad into the trash.

He was damned if he did, and damned if he didn't. Resting hadn't helped so far, maybe the only option was to go under the knife and risk it all. His shoulders tensed, his thighs bunched and his hands clenched into fists. Tension stole his breath. This was his own fault. He'd heard stories of singers losing it all when they overworked their voice. His vanity had refused to consider he might be fallible or weak enough to succumb to physical failure. How could he gamble with his future? How could he not?

Initially, his agent had encouraged him to tour as much as possible to build his fame. Album followed album. Concerts came too closely together. He could have backed off at any time, but he loved the limelight. Concerts were his lifeblood. It'd been years since his shows failed to sell out. His agent encouraged him to do more shows on the certainty he'd continue to sell out and make them both more money.

Damn!

This was his fault. He should have taken it easier.

He'd stolen away in the middle of the night leaving Steph behind. She'd have come with him, if he had asked. Instead he was alone again. Served him right. Damn his stupid, selfish hide.

He paced the room, three steps left, turn, three steps right, turn. Back and forth. The options sucked. It was either take years off his career and lose the spotlight and hope to return, if he healed, or get the surgery now and hope for the best. When push came to shove he had no damned choice.

∽

TUCKER ACCOMPANIED Brett to the hospital. The doctor brought them in through the staff entrance and they snuck to the surgical ward and right into a private room. During check-in the doctor explained Brett had been assigned a private male nurse who didn't care for country music, to avoid the complication of a star-struck fan. It wasn't that females couldn't be trusted, but the doctor had worked with several stars and knew how quickly word spread. Consequently, he had staff members designated for dealing with famous patients. A major factor in maintaining privacy was choosing staff who had no interest in the involved celebrity. Brett was barely in his room when his nurse, Gary, showed up and handed him a gown and slippers.

"You can hang your clothing in the closet. We recommend you give your valuables, wallet, hat, boots and the like, to your friend for safekeeping. Undress completely and slip into this gown and we'll be ready for you in no time."

"That's it. I'm out." Tucker laughed. "I'm not hanging around to stare at your ass. Give me your wallet."

Brett handed it over but refused to part with his hat and boots. "No way. I keep my boots and my hat. I need some dignity."

Brett clenched his gown closed behind his back with one hand and straightened his Stetson with the other. His boxer-briefs felt insubstantial and unfit to cover his backside. Seriously, why did he have to be nearly naked? This was oral surgery, in through his mouth. You'd think they'd let him have pajama bottoms at least. He glared at Gary when he returned, wheeling a blood pressure machine.

"I need some damned pants. My ass is freezing." He clomped across the room, his cowboy boots stumping with every step.

The nurse pivoted at the sound. "You've got your boots and hat on? Dude, this ain't no rodeo. Lose the fancy duds and put your slippers on. Please."

"Those stupid paper ones? Who the hell designed these. I'll keep my boots."

The nurse shook his head. "Mr. Wyatt, you don't want to ruin those boots by wearing them into surgery. Nor would you want to contaminate the operating theater. Once we get you settled, I'll find you some pajamas."

"Step on it," Brett demanded.

"Mr. Wyatt, I understand you've got a lot on the line here. But don't worry, we'll take care of you."

"A lot on the line?" Brett's blood pressure skyrocketed. "My entire life is on the line. This could spell the end of my career. How would you feel in my place?" He crossed his arms over his chest and glared. A breeze whipped across his back, deepening the chill fear running through him. He grasped the flaps of his gown and clenched them in his fist, concealing his backside.

"This is a relatively minor surgery. The doctor went over the risks with you. Complications are rare, less than one percent. You've got a ninety-nine percent chance of pulling through this unscathed. Generally, patients come out better than they went in. It's going to be okay. Now come over here and sit down. I'll get your vitals and we'll get this show on the road."

"It's my vitals I'm worried about," Brett complained. "My ass is freezing and my voice is all I have." He flopped into the bedside chair. "Get it over with."

Gary placed a hand on his shoulder and squeezed. "This is going to be okay. You'll come through just fine. You're in the care of the country's leading ENT surgeon. This is the best place for you. Relax, man."

Shame flooded through Brett. Gary was probably right. He had no other option and there was no sense being a stubborn mule about this. Time to suck it up and get over himself.

"Sorry. I'm tense. I've got a lot riding on this, but I shouldn't take it out on you. I apologize. I'll try and rein in my panic." He drew in a slow, calming breath.

"Apology accepted. Now, think of something calm and relaxing, we need to lower your blood pressure before you blow a gasket."

Eventually, his vitals were completed.

"Now, put your hat and boots into the closet. They'll be safe there. Your friend hired a plainclothes guard to sit outside your door and keep away the curious. They'll watch your possessions, too."

Brett complied without complaint.

"Hop onto the bed and the orderly will take you to the OR."

"Is there any sense in insisting I walk?"

"None. Hospital policy."

Brett lowered himself into the bed without comment.

∼

After four interminable days in the hospital, Brett was released. Two weeks post surgery, he had a follow up with the doctor. Now, he sat in front of a blazing fire, staring out the window of his condo. Rain poured from dismal gray skies. The fire warmed his body but did nothing to chase away the chill in his soul. He debated the merits of hurling himself out the window. Where did he go from here? His career was over? He had nothing left.

Goddamn. Dammit-all-to-hell.

As a rule, Brett didn't curse much. But this time, no other word would suffice.

He didn't harbor suicidal thoughts, just this-crap-will-never-get-better viewpoint. Like all things, he'd get beyond this, but right here, right now, he had no idea how. The fact that he'd dumped Steph without word meant he couldn't even call her.

From the moment his voice cracked at his last concert, nothing had gone right. Everything that could possibly go wrong had. Complications with the anesthetic, too much scarring, and a follow-up infection meant he'd probably never sing in concert again. Ever. His vocal cords were damaged beyond repair. So much for Gary's insistence he'd be fine. Brett should have known better. His glory days were over and fate was handing him a crap deal.

He might, in time, with proper rest and rehab, sing again, but touring and concerts were done. Forever. The doctor was optimistic a recording career, taken slow and easy might be feasible; after rehab. But, that was the same doctor who had said complications were rare.

His occupational, rehabilitation therapist had been by earlier and had put Brett through his paces. Just looking at her annoyed him and he was sick of the word rehab. Nobody understood what he was going through and he had no one to talk to. He threw his drink at the fireplace. Glass exploded everywhere and the alcohol poofed into flames, scorching the picture frames on the mantle.

Shit!

He leapt to his feet and snatched the pictures out of harm's way. He'd nearly destroyed a collage of images of him and Elijah. The frame was scorched, but the picture was intact. He'd never have forgiven himself if he had wrecked it. On the other corner of the mantle, the popsicle stick house Elijah had made him stood undamaged by his carelessness. Damn, he had to get a grip on himself. He gently set the picture in a safe spot on the glossy black grand piano across the room, beside his treasure basket.

The basket held a clay dragon that looked more like a lopsided dog with wings, a braided string bolo tie, a stack of snapshots of Elijah, his family and Brett relaxing at the beach and the leather key fob Elijah had made him. It matched his wallet. Every single item related to Elijah held a special place in his heart. They were irreplaceable. He picked up the fob and grabbed another glass from the bar.

Fresh drink in hand, he perched on the edge of the couch and sank into misery. He'd cuss a blue streak if his voice worked.

CHAPTER 12

Barely able to keep from thinking about Brett, Steph tried her best to bury herself in bookkeeping. The band was gone and life had settled to normal. New guests were scheduled to arrive in the morning. She just had to turn her mind to something functional and forget she'd ever met Brett Wyatt. He hadn't contacted her in weeks. Tucker said he was having surgery, but that was weeks ago. Anger flushed her cheeks. He could have had the decency to let her know how the surgery went. And Tucker was no better. He'd taken off, too. Either one of them could have left a note.

Brett was a no-good rotten turncoat. He'd ditched her without a goodbye. She knew their relationship wasn't long term; but even one-night guests let her know they were leaving. She'd known his leaving would hurt, but not like this. If he was here right now, she'd give him a piece of her mind. He'd get a dressing-down he wouldn't soon forget.

As if! She flopped back in her chair and tossed her pen on the desk. Yeah, she was annoyed at him, but she really wanted to know how the surgery had gone. Tucker should have called. Maybe she should call him. No, it smacked of desperation and she wouldn't be that woman. She wouldn't chase him no matter how concerned she was.

Why hadn't Tucker called?

There'd been nothing in the papers or tabloids and nothing had leaked to the internet. It was like he'd just stepped off the face of the earth. How did a superstar just disappear?

"Howdy, boss." Penny stood in the office doorway. "Any word on our boy?"

"Nothing yet. You'd think he'd have called by now." Bitterness laced her voice. She hated herself when she was like this. "I could have gone with him."

"You?" Penny laughed lightly. "You can barely visit Okotoks and Calgary, let alone brave Toronto again. I get the sentiment though. You want to be there for him, even though he acted like a colossal turd. You've got a big heart."

"He was scared." She tried to defend him, but she didn't believe her own words.

"Probably, that doesn't make it okay to be a dick. JT's totally pissed at him. You're not the only one who wasn't filled in. Nobody but Tucker knew what was going on. I say take him out behind the woodshed and put a switch to his backside. That's what they'd do in the Old West."

"Dueling six-shooters at dawn?" The corners of Steph's smile turned up a bit. "I'd rather tip the outhouse with him in it." Her lips quirked into a genuine grin.

"That would be a great revenge. Picture the headlines, "Country Superstar Covered in Crap." Her laugh echoed off the ceiling and lightened Steph's heartache.

"In my dreams." She chuckled.

The phone jangled on the desk. Penny waved toward it. "I'll leave you to it. I'm off to make cinnamon buns for breakfast tomorrow."

"Thanks." She picked up the phone. "Wild Rose Inn, this is Steph. How can I help you?"

"You need to come to Toronto." Tucker's words were as much an order as a suggestion.

"Indeed? Why would I want to do that? I don't fly anymore. And I avoid Ontario like the plague." Her heart thundered in her chest. Did Brett need her?

"Brett's a wreck. He's not eating. He's drinking too much."

"Oh, no. What's wrong?" Tension squeezed her chest.

"I can't tell you. I promised I wouldn't. Just trust me on this. He needs you. He's asked about you several times. I said I haven't talked to you."

"You haven't called since you left. I've been here dying to know how the surgery went. You never called, not even once. You didn't email or text either." She bit her lip to halt the accusatory flow of words.

"Fine. I'm trying to balance two friendships here. Brett and you. I promised I wouldn't call you. I'm breaking my word to him. I can't tell you what's up. Just trust me and get your ass out here. He won't talk to his family and I only get in because I have a key. There's a ticket booked in your name for the nine-a.m. flight on WestJet. Be on it. I'll pick you up at the airport." He hung up before she could object.

She replaced the receiver and bunched her hands into fists to still the shaking. She couldn't do this. No way. No how. Leave her sanctuary and return to Toronto, the place where her life hit the skids and deteriorated in front of her eyes? Her guts clenched, and she swallowed a gag and an incipient panic attack.

She gripped the desk tightly with both hands, white-knuckled, until her fingers cramped. She rubbed them on her thighs to relieve the ache. A headache loomed and negative thoughts pushed their way past carefully erected barriers.

She leaped to her feet and clapped her hands together in agitation while sucking in deep breaths. She would not succumb to panic or depression. She could handle this. She'd been working with a therapist on this since just after the accident. She had the skills, she just had to reach deep and find them. Travelling never used to be an issue for her.

She stopped in her tracks, hands dropping to her sides. Why should she go? He'd ditched her without warning. Not a call, note, or letter. Not even a text message. He didn't deserve to have her rush to his side.

If he wasn't seeing his family or Tucker, he was alone. Tucker hadn't told her what the issue was, but she'd done her research; his voice could be gone. Temporarily, permanently. Either would cripple Brett mentally and emotionally. During his stay, she'd learned music was everything to him.

How could she leave him alone?

How could she go?

She trundled out of her office and shuffled around the main floor rubbing her hands together and running options through her mind. She stared at the couch in the entertainment room where she'd sat with Brett and Tucker, rediscovering their joy in Elijah. Unfortunately, there were only two options, go to him or leave him be. She wandered out of the room, pausing to straighten a picture or knickknack here and there.

"What am I going to do?" she mumbled to a bouquet of carnations on the hall table.

"About what?" Penny leaned against the kitchen doorjamb. "I assume this is related to the phone call." She watched Steph pace for a moment. "This really has you agitated. Spill, sister."

"That was Tucker. He won't tell me anything; except Brett needs me. He's refusing to see anyone, even his family. Tucker basically forces himself into Brett's suite. He thinks I should go to Brett; see if I can help him."

"So, without knowing what's happening, or what the *issue* is, you're supposed to drop everything and run to a man who ditched you without saying goodbye? That's freaking bold. It takes a lot of nerve to request such an enormous favor."

"Brett's not asking, Tucker is. You know how far back Tucker and I go. We've been through a lot together. He stood by me when the media was set to crucify me. Any other parent would blame me. I owe him."

"And do you owe Brett?"

"No." She sagged into herself. Put that way, it was so simple. She owed him nothing; not one single moment of her time. "I wonder if I owe it to myself to go. To confront my fears and try to move beyond them. If he really does need me, I'd like to be there."

"Woman, you're insane. I'd never give him a second thought. He burned you. He didn't give a crap how you felt when he walked away. Why should you care about him?"

Penny was playing devil's advocate. She had a way of prodding until you saw a situation from more than one side and it was extremely annoying. Steph sighed and rubbed her neck. It was stiff enough she could hardly move her head.

"That's just it. I shouldn't care. I don't want to care; but I do." She stared at the floor, eyes watering. "I do care."

"Do you love him?"

She glanced up in shock. Penny leaned against the wall, ankles crossed, arms folded over her chest and a knowing look on her face. "Don't even try to lie to me. I know you better than that."

"I don't know."

"Liar." She walked over and embraced Steph. "Don't lie to me, or to yourself. Dig deep. If you didn't love him, you wouldn't even consider going to him."

Steph crumpled into Penny's arms, holding tight. "I don't know. What if he doesn't want me?"

"What if he does?" She patted Steph's back and stepped away. "Will you be able to forgive yourself if you don't at least try?"

"You know, you're freaking annoying?" Steph tried to glare; but a half-smile curled the corners of her mouth up. "I want to go. He was, is, important to me. I just don't know if I can."

Penny's laugh startled her. "Girl, you can do anything for the man you love. Love gives us power."

"I didn't say I loved him."

"You didn't have to." She turned Steph toward the stairs and gave her a little shove. "Go. Pack. Start visualizing yourself getting through this without trouble."

Eighteen hours later, she stood at the gate wondering if she'd be able to board her flight. Nobody had noticed her so far and she was doing her best to keep a low profile. But what about when she arrived in Toronto? Would anyone recognize her? Or was her fifteen minutes of fame finally over?

A flight attendant approached her. "You look nervous. Anything I can help you with?"

"Um. No. Thanks. It's just that I'm facing a personal—issue. I'm not sure I can handle it."

"Those are the worst. I've dealt with my share. It's not much comfort, I know, but this airline has an outstanding safety record. Is someone meeting you?"

"Yeah, an old friend."

"A safe plane, an old friend. Maybe this'll work out okay for you." She smiled broadly. "If you board last, it'll reduce the sitting and waiting time. Less time to fret is probably a good thing. Let someone know if you need a pep talk on the flight."

A few sentences from a stranger, combined with not being recognized, calmed her nerves. She was still a wreck, but at least now she knew she could board the flight. She watched everyone else board the plane, fighting her urge to cut and run.

A woman and small boy raced to the check-in counter. "We're not late, are we?"

"Not at all." The attendant smiled at her. "It's just you two and this lady left to board. In minutes, you'll be airborne and on your way."

"Let's go, Mom." The redheaded boy pulled on his mother's arm.

The attendant checked their boarding passes, waved them bon voyage, and then nodded encouragingly at Steph.

They hustled to their seats, and Steph settled in on the aisle seat with the boy between Steph and his mother.

"I'm Nick." He grinned at Steph. "We're going to see my dad. He's a doctor and he makes sick people better. He gots a new job, in Toronna."

"Toronto," his mother corrected. "Leave the lady alone and buckle up, Nick."

"It's okay. I could use the distraction," Steph confessed, fastening her belt.

"Nervous flyer?"

"No, I'm just not looking forward to my destination. A lot of bad memories for me. But a friend needs me, even if he won't admit it."

"Good for you for facing your fears." Nick's mother patted Steph's hand. "The world needs more people like you, willing to get out of their comfort zone to help others. You should feel proud."

Heat rose in Steph's face and she glanced away. "Thank you." She turned and smiled. She did feel proud of herself for facing her fears.

She'd made it through the Calgary airport and onto the plane unscathed; now all she had to do was get through Toronto without being spotted and then she'd be scot-free. Until it was time to brave the public eye again.

∾

Tucker was there, as promised, when she landed. He whisked her through the crowd to his pickup.

"What kind of truck is this? Vehicles aren't my thing."

"2017 Ford Raptor. I got a heck of a deal on it and gave Anita the Beemer. She's more about the status and I was done with it."

"You gave your ex a car?" She laughed when he shrugged the question off. "Tell me about Brett."

"I can't. I swear to God I want to and I would if I could. I'm already breaking my word by calling you and bringing you here. But, he's in a funk and something has to rattle him loose. You've been there, you understand how the hole just keeps getting deeper unless you find something to hold onto to pull yourself out with."

Gosh, did she ever know about that. Two years after her mental crash, she was still seeing a shrink. Things were better now, but she still had days…

"And my role is?" It wasn't a light question. She needed to know how Tucker thought she could help. A lot of depressed people chose to wallow in their misery without trying to shake it off. For some, it was a choice, for others, they just didn't know how to start the climb.

"Talk to him. Support him. But mostly, just listen to him without judgment. He's had a pretty easy life without issues. This vocal cord thing has knocked him for a loop and I don't think he can climb out alone. You've been there. You know what it's like."

"So do you."

"He's not hearing me. He barely lets me into his suite. He cares for you, and I think that may make the difference."

The ride to Brett's condo was interminable. She enjoyed Tucker's company and their conversation, but the forty-five-minute drive felt like hours. Nothing like fear and uncertainty to turn time endless.

Tucker unlocked the condo and they stepped inside. The sound of furniture crashing and glass breaking exploded through the entry. "Shit." Tucker growled and motioned for her to follow him inside.

They found Brett, sprawled on the floor beside an overturned coffee table; shards of glass littered the hardwood floor.

"Where's the broom?" Steph asked.

"What the hell is she doing here? Get out. Both of you." His words were slurred and his voice was pitched low, and all the more intense for it.

"Suck it up, Wyatt. I flew all this way, I'm not leaving just because you're having a hissy fit." Whoa! Where had that come from? She glanced at Tucker who looked impressed. Brett just growled and tried to crawl away.

"Don't move until I clean up the glass. You're going to cut yourself." Thankfully, he sat on the floor, head hung low, chin on his chest, hands fisted in his hair. She stared a moment. Tucker was right, this man was broken and needed an intervention.

Tucker disappeared and returned with a wet-dry vacuum.

"Climb up on the couch until I get this mess cleaned up. It smells like a distillery in here. Are you drinking this early in the day? Are you insane?" She glared at him.

"My life, not yours," he grumbled and climbed up off the floor.

She made short work of the mess and turned to Tucker. "We're good. You don't have to stay if you don't want to."

"Go on, get out of here, you turncoat. We don't need you."

Steph stifled a smile. He'd aligned himself with her without even knowing it. She waved to Tucker, shooing him toward the door. "I'll call you if I need you." Tucker left and she heard the deadbolt click behind him.

"Want to talk?"

"No. I'm going to bed." He grabbed a half-empty bottle of whiskey off the end table and staggered to his feet.

"I'll take that." She snatched the bottle out of his hands. "No booze until you talk to me."

His glare could have cut steel; but he staggered down a hallway, presumably toward the bedroom without complaint. She watched him go, one hand on her hip, the other clutching the bottle until her fingers cramped.

She looked around his suite. He'd been right, it was big; and it was filthy. She gave herself a tour. The entry came into the middle of the apartment. The enormous living room, where she'd found him, was to the left and came complete with a grand piano. The kitchen and dining areas were to the right of the door. Beyond that was a hallway leading to a music studio and a room designed as a home theater and a luxurious bathroom.

Back the other way, down the hallway Brett had taken, was a bathroom and four suites with their own baths. The last door, closed tight must be the master bedroom. Everywhere she looked, the place was a disaster. Empty booze bottles and take-out containers littered every flat surface. He must be eating take-out three times a day. Or else he'd had a party. Dirty laundry had been dropped and left where it landed. She was surprised he'd even changed.

She returned to the kitchen and started cleaning. She couldn't stay in a dump like this. Was it always this filthy, or had this disaster spawned in the week since his surgery? She shrugged the thought off. First things first. Clean up and get rid of the booze.

One of the bedrooms, the cleanest one, had a locking door. She'd noticed it on her tour. She'd hide the booze in there and claim the room as her own. She tidied, straightened, vacuumed and polished until the place shone like a show-suite. She opened the windows to blow out the stale booze-laden air. Finally, she unpacked her bag and tucked it into the closet alongside the booze she'd collected. She stacked the garbage and empty bottles beside the door to take out later, once she knew where they went.

She grabbed a mystery novel off the shelf in her bedroom and returned to the living room. She stepped through the French doors onto a rooftop patio. Lush and green, it was an oasis of calm after the storm inside the apartment. She settled into a plush chair in dappled sunlight to read until Brett came out. She'd let him sleep it off. Maybe he'd be more civil after a long rest.

He didn't surface until she was fixing herself eggs and toast the next morning.

"Hi." His voice was low and hoarse. He slid onto a stool at the breakfast bar facing the counter. He'd showered and combed his hair; but his sweats and T-shirt were ragged and stained. They must be comfort clothes, because they were fit for the trash. Were men like women? Did they keep old favorites for rough days?

"Good morning. Coffee?" She filled her voice with sunshine.

"Yes."

"I beg your pardon?"

"Yes. Coffee."

"Tsk. Tsk. Manners?"

"My house, my coffee. Pour."

She grabbed the pot and held it over the sink, dribbling the liquid black-gold into the drain. "I'll pour all right."

"Coffee. Please." One corner of his mouth twitched.

She poured him a cup and added cream and sugar. "Here you go. Do you need something for your headache?" She placed a glass of ice water beside the coffee he clutched in his hand.

"Yes. Please. In the cupboard above the fridge."

She placed the over-the-counter pain tablets and his bottle of antibiotics in front of him. "You shouldn't take these with alcohol. You never mix booze and drugs. It can cause bad reactions. Sometimes, alcohol makes drugs less effective." She paused and blundered right into dangerous territory.

"I gather from the prescription pain medication and the antibiotics the surgery didn't go well." She buttered the toast when it popped and slid the plate in front of him.

He stared at the eggs, toast and orange slices like they were a plate of maggots.

"Eat it. You need sustenance to counteract the booze. Your body won't heal if you don't feed it."

He picked up the fork and took a small, grudging bite.

Steph turned her back to hide her grin. Small victories. She busied herself making another breakfast. By the time she sat on the stool beside him, his plate was empty and his coffee finished. "More coffee?"

"I can get it." He paused. "Thank you for breakfast." He rinsed his plate and put it in the dishwasher, poured another coffee and topped up her mug. "I'm going outside."

She let him go without comment. At least he was being semi-civil and he'd cleaned up after himself. She cuddled the small achievement to her chest. His body was probably still soaked in booze, but he hadn't asked for a drink. She'd pester him to talk after she finished eating.

∽

BRETT PACED circles on the patio. He puttered around plucking off dead flowers and leaves before he started watering plants. Why had she come? Why had she cleaned up? He'd kill Tucker for bringing her here. He swept the walkway and fluffed the cushions on the patio furniture. He was mostly sober now, but if he didn't keep busy, he'd head inside for another drink. His life was ruined. Drowning in alcohol didn't seem such a bad way to go.

Where was she?

Finally, she wandered out onto the patio in pink flowery shorts, a lacy T-shirt and sandals, holding a novel in her hand. "Mind if I read out here?"

Her legs were as glorious as he remembered. He could almost feel them wrapped around his waist. He pushed the image aside and answered her. "You can read wherever you want. Aren't you going to nag me into talking?" Anger laced his voice. Damn. This wasn't her fault. Why was he snapping at her?

"Do you want to talk?" She sat on the swing and set it rocking with a light push of her foot.

God, she was beautiful. His mind hadn't been playing tricks on him since he left. She was lovely, even with one eyebrow raised, mocking him without words.

"No. I just want to be here, without anyone bothering me." He winced internally. He was being an ass.

"Okay. I'll just read." She cracked open the book and looked at him. "But if you would like to chat, I'll listen."

He stared at her as she delved into the book. There was no judgment, no censure in her voice. Wasn't she going to give him hell for the mess? For being drunk? His mother would have torn a strip the size of the 401 Highway off his ass.

She sat there, reading, totally ignoring him. He paced the patio, bigger than a lot of urban backyards. She read and read some more, without looking at him once. He finished his coffee. He paused beside her on his way inside to make another pot.

"Would you like more coffee?" God, why was he starting a conversation.

"I'd love another cup. I left my mug beside the sink. Black, please."

"Baileys?"

She raised one eyebrow, but her smile never faded. "No, thank you."

And just like that, three words, and he was slapped down. Where did women learn that shit? They must be born knowing it. Every woman he'd ever dated had it down pat. Right then, she reminded him so much of his mother he wanted to slither into a hole and hide.

Guilt crawled down his spine and made his guts clench. His mother would be worried. He'd better call her soon. She'd left dozens of messages on his machine. He'd listened to them all.

Inside, he started coffee and picked up the kitchen phone. He punched in his parents' home number and waited for it to ring. Half a ring in, the ringing cut off.

"Brett, I'm so glad you called." His mother's panicked voice flowed over him like a soothing balm. "Are you okay? How was your operation?"

"Hi, Mom. The surgery sucked." He cleared his throat. "There were complications. I don't want to talk about it. I just wanted to tell you I'm alive." Cutting her off and giving non-answers hurt more than he wanted to admit.

"But—"

"I need time, Mom. Time to think and plan. I'll never give another concert." His voice warbled with unshed tears.

"Never? That's terrible. You're such a wonderful singer. I have all your CDs. You shouldn't be alone. I'll come right over."

"Mom. Please. I just need to be alone." *She had all his CDs? When had she started listening to his music?* He pushed the thought away. That was a puzzle for another time; for when his world wasn't falling apart.

"You need someone to talk to."

"I have—a friend here. She'll listen when I need to talk."

"A woman? Is it serious? Who is she?" Her voiced picked up with excitement.

"She's just a friend. I have to go. I just wanted to let you know I'm surviving. I love you, Mom. Tell Dad I said hi and pass the word on that I'll call everyone back. Eventually."

"Oh, darling," she crooned. "If you're sure—but call me if you need anything. Please." The last word rent his heart in two.

"Thanks, Mom. I love you. Bye." He hung up without waiting for her response. He grabbed a tissue from the box that had appeared on the counter while he was asleep. Steph. He wiped his eyes and blew his nose.

He poured their coffees and returned to the patio. He paused in the doorway, studying the way the sun lit the dark, breeze-ruffled strands of her hair. It shone with flashes of red, gold and golden brown. She smiled up at him and a bit of peace stole into his heart. She'd come for him. He smiled and her smile blossomed into a beautiful heart-splitting grin.

"Welcome back."

He set her coffee on the table at her elbow and sat on the other end of the swing, his mug cupped between his hands. Did she mean welcome back to the patio? It sounded like more.

"Did I hear voices? I couldn't make out words, I just thought I heard talking?"

He nodded. "I called Mom to tell her I'm okay. She's been calling." The heat of shame burned his cheeks.

"That'll ease her worries. Mothers do fret."

"Not just mothers," he conceded. "Friends, too." He brushed one finger down her cheek.

"Friends, too. Thanks for the coffee." She toasted him with the cup.

They sat in silence; he kept the swing moving with a slow, easy motion and she stared at the sky.

She pointed toward a cloud. "Oh, look. A dragon."

"I don't see it."

"What do you see?"

"A Saint Bernard?"

"With wings? You're off your rocker." She laughed.

"Not off my rocker, but not entirely sane either," he replied soberly.

She made a sound of agreement. "Life's hard knocks do that to you." She pointed again. "Is that a guitar?"

"Not just any guitar, it's Willie Nelson's classic Martin N-20 guitar. Willie sure could play." He sounded envious, but he couldn't help himself.

"I've heard you pick a tune or two. And I've seen the guitar collection behind glass in the music room. Pretty impressive stuff. What's with the one in the display all by itself?"

The question cut deep. "That's my first guitar. I bought it with money from my paper route. How corny is that?" Why did he tell her? He could have given any lame excuse.

"Wow. Can I touch it?"

She actually sounded impressed, although he couldn't understand why. It was just a guitar, and unimportant to anyone but him. "Why?"

"Come on, Brett, you're an icon. If I could say I touched your guitar and had a picture… my friends would die with envy." Her laugh tickled down his spine.

"Now?"

She dropped her novel and mug onto the table, leaped to her feet and clapped her hands. "Oh, yes. Please."

Her enthusiasm, as she raced to the music room, was infectious. He caught up to her standing in front of the case, hands behind her back and an enormous smile on her face. He pulled out the guitar; a tremor of melancholy passed over him as he handed it to her.

She settled on the couch with the guitar in her lap. She handed him her phone. "A picture, please." He snapped several and sat beside her. He positioned the guitar properly and showed her how to hold it. He slung one arm around her and the guitar to show her how to strum. She smiled up at him like he'd given her the moon. He snapped a picture of them together with the guitar.

"Proof you held my guitar." He managed a weak smile.

She leaned in and kissed him on the cheek. "Thank you, Brett. This means a lot to me." She fumbled around and tried to play, her head tipped to the side, her lips pursed in concentration and her brows bunched together. He guided her hands and showed her a simple chord and rhythm.

She tried a few times and laughed at herself before she smiled again and sighed blissfully. "Can you play for me? Please?"

Every bit of his body and soul rebelled at the request. He wanted to throw the guitar and smash it to bits. But the please in her soft, sexy voice moved him more than he wanted to admit. He took the guitar and tuned it quickly and efficiently.

She slid off the couch and kneeled in front of him, her expression rapt; a pleased smile wreathed her face and lit her eyes. Damn. He swallowed a lump of emotion. Fear? Sadness? Regret? Happiness? He'd be damned if he could classify what he was feeling.

He started strumming, low at first and gradually growing louder. He didn't sing, the tune had no words. He had no words. It was an expression of the confusion in his soul. Of all he'd lost and would never have again. It echoed his joy in having her here, without pressure to talk or reveal his agony. He played until his emotions ebbed and there was nothing left but a big hollow in his heart and soul.

"That was beautiful." Her voice wavered.

He glanced up; tears streamed down her face and dripped off her chin. She didn't hide them, she didn't look away. She granted him a watery smile and set down her phone.

Her phone?

"You didn't?"

"Record it? I did, from the first notes. I won't share it with anyone. I'll delete it if you want. But, it's so beautiful, so poignant, I can't even count the emotions I heard. You bared your soul to me." She sniffed loudly. "It's new, right?"

Geez. It was new. He did that? He hadn't written a note in years, except the few scribbles while he was at the inn. With her. "Um. Don't delete it just yet."

"I can send it to you?" It was both a statement and a question.

He couldn't find the words to answer, he just nodded. He hadn't intended to compose, it had just happened and it was good. Very good. He might never share it, but with her recording as he played, he could transcribe it if he ever chose to. There was no way he'd ever recreate it unassisted. Some pieces were planned and executed, others, like this one, just came to you. He rose slowly and tucked the guitar in its display case. He trailed his fingers over its curves, grateful it had given him this moment of peace and creativity. He owed Steph for that. Deep inside, he wondered if she'd manipulated him into playing; but for the life of him, he didn't care. His muse may have paused for a visit, but it didn't solve anything. He still couldn't sing.

He walked away without turning back. Guilt, pain and self-recrimination barked at his heels as he fled the room that was once his favorite place. Without singing, he was nothing.

CHAPTER 13

Steph watched him go. Torn between the desire to comfort him and the knowledge that he needed to be alone, she made no move to stop him. Solitude was part of the healing process, just not too much of it. Getting him to play as an emotional release had popped into her mind out of nowhere.

Therapy had taught her creativity was a great outlet for stress. She'd made God-awful clay figures; her grade one students could have done better work. But she had banged out her emotions in the malleable clay. She kept a few pieces hidden away as reminders of her healing journey. Eventually, she'd turned to knitting and quilting. There was something incredibly soothing about the repetitive actions. She wasn't good at either, yet. They required just enough concentration to distract her while her subconscious mind worked out her problems and that was satisfaction enough.

The emotion he poured out through his music was unlike anything she'd ever encountered. They said music spoke louder than words; she'd doubted that before now. Sure, a talented musician could work your emotions, but not like this. He'd devastated her and showed flickers of joy amid the melancholy; creating a rollercoaster of emotion. He hadn't shared words, or the demons he'd faced, but he'd given his emotions. It was a start.

Instinct told her this wasn't a temporary setback. His surgery had the earmarks of a life-changing event. If the damage was too great he might never sing again, even casually. She dashed away tears. He must be going through Hell. Forcing him to talk wouldn't work. She'd have to be patient and understanding and bide her time. Until then, she had to get out of this condo or go nuts. She wasn't used to being cooped up all day.

She googled the closest grocery store on her phone, slapped on a ball cap, grabbed the keys she had found yesterday and headed out. She was taking a risk of being noticed, but they needed milk and a few others things, and she needed to breathe. The patio was fabulous, but too small compared to the vast expanse of the ranch.

Downstairs, she paused to chat with Edgar, the doorman. Tucker had introduced them when she had arrived. Edgar was pushing seventy-five, but he was strong and fit. His suit was perfectly pressed and his gray hair neat and tidy. He was the picture of a gentleman and deadly serious about building security.

"How is Mr. Wyatt feeling after his surgery?"

"Excuse me?" She stared at him, knowing he'd read the shock on her face.

"He told me about it himself and I talked to Mr. Marcus when he left yesterday. Don't worry," he said with a wink. "I won't breathe a word about it to anyone. You needn't bother answering if it makes you uncomfortable."

"Thank you. Mr. Wyatt was doing just fine when I saw him this morning." After a few minutes of small talk, she confirmed she'd be able to get in without trouble.

"When should I expect you back?" The enquiry was polite.

"Half an hour? Forty-five minutes. I'm just running to the grocery store."

The sun was bright and warm, though a chill breeze fluttered around the skyscrapers around her. She shivered. Why would anyone want to live in the city? In the past two years, she'd come to wonder why she'd ever chosen city life. Small town living was definitely more her style.

The grocery store was blessedly quiet and warm. She grabbed a few essentials and started back toward the condo. She rounded the last corner and walked smack dab into mayhem. Seven news vans cluttered the street and the sidewalk in front of the building was packed with reporters and camera crews. She backed up, bumping into two pedestrians and leaned against the wall around the corner.

Somehow, Brett's surgery must have made it to the news. What else would explain the circus she'd just witnessed? Maybe another celebrity lived in the building. It was very high-end.

She hustled back half a block and slipped inside a Tim Hortons. Coffee and muffin in hand, she huddled into the corner and waited for the crowd to disperse. Over the next two hours, she checked on the crowd every twenty minutes and then returned to her seat.

"Excuse me. Aren't you the teacher in the scandal with the boy who died a few years ago?"

She glanced up. A tall, suited man stood beside her table. Crap. She never should have left the building.

"I'm sorry, you must be mistaken." She shook her head and did her best to look innocent and bewildered.

"No. I know you. I tried to interview you." He snapped his fingers in her face. "Sally—Sarah—Stephanie something. Ah, I know… That boy in your class died."

She swallowed a lump of fear and clenched her hands to still their shaking. She had to get out of here before he realized he was right. All it would take was a single shout and she'd have a swarm of reporters hounding her and tearing her to bits like a pack of rabid hounds. Not this time! No way. She was out of here.

She grabbed her bag and pushed past him. "I have no idea what you're talking about. Excuse me. I have to go."

She raced out the door, swerved right to avoid a mother and

stroller. She bolted as fast as her feet could carry her, with the reporter hollering after her. She dipped around the corner right into the arms of another reporter. Crap. Panic had driven her straight to the mob.

"Grab her. That's Stephanie Alexander, the teacher who let a student die in the pool."

The crowd immediately turned and swarmed her. What had she been thinking? She never should have come to Toronto.

She shoved one reporter away and elbowed two more, pushing her way forward with as much ferocity as she could muster. Someone grabbed her grocery bag, another grabbed her purse, trying to slow her progress toward the door. She dropped the bag and punched wildly at the woman holding her purse, landing a solid blow and sending the woman's glasses flying. Fists flailing, knees and feet flying, she fought through the crowd. She'd have made MMA fighter, Georges St. Pierre, proud.

They pushed and shoved until she was pressed against the wall, just a step away from the door. Bright lights blinded her eyes and microphones smacked into her face as the crowd jostled to get closer. Tears threatened and she battled them back.

No! This wasn't happening again. They'd destroyed her once. Never again.

"Shut up," she shouted. "Yes, a boy died on my watch. The fault wasn't mine. I saved six kids from drowning that day. If you want to find someone to blame and pester, talk to the pool management who authorized cutbacks and cheated on maintenance. I have nothing else to say, now get out of my way before someone gets hurt."

"Steph!"

She turned her head toward the hoarse cry. Brett stood in the half-open door waving at her. "Over here. Come inside."

The crowd abandoned her and swarmed him.

"No!" He didn't need this. Not now, not so soon after surgery.

He held up a hand; the crowd quieted instantly. "Leave her

alone. Get out of her way." The crowd backed away and she hurried toward him. "If any of you ever hassle this woman again, you'll never get another quote, interview or photograph from me. Is that clear?"

He drew her to his side. "Are you okay?"

"I'm fine." She swallowed hard, biting back the truth. She was shaken to her core by reliving her worst nightmare. His eyes were soft and understanding.

He looked up at the crowd. "I know you're here for me. Leave Miss Alexander alone." He glared at the reporters, one after another, until they'd all taken a small step back. "I have nothing to say at this time. I'm asking you to leave and stop blocking traffic and annoying innocent civilians. There'll be a press conference soon. Until then, go back to your newsrooms. That's it for today."

He ushered her inside, leaving the grumbling crowd behind.

"I'm sorry, Miss Alexander," the doorman said. "I wanted to warn you as soon as the crowd showed up. I don't have your phone number; so I called Mr. Wyatt. Next thing I knew he was down here. In his bare feet, too!" He stared at the floor, wringing his hands. "Nothing like this has ever happened on my watch." He looked up, his eyes begged for understanding.

"It's okay, Edgar. No harm done." *God, if only that were true.*

"I doubt that, miss. I'm ever so sorry this happened to you." He followed them to the elevator.

She paused at the doors and turned to him. "You can't change the media. You tried to warn me and I should have known better than to risk a trip outside. I'm fine. Perfectly fine." She leaned over and kissed him on the cheek. "Everything's okay."

The elevator chimed, the doors slid open and they backed inside.

"It's okay, Edgar. We're both fine," Brett reassured the man as the doors swished shut.

CHAPTER 14

Brett turned toward her and grasped her shoulders.

"What the hell were you thinking? Why did you leave?" He shook her lightly. "I nearly shit myself when Edgar called. Why didn't you take your cell phone?"

She shoved his hands off her shoulders and backed up against the far wall. "You needed groceries. I went to the stupid store."

"Oh, honey. I have a service for that." He reached out for her.

She batted his hand away. "Don't. How would I know you have a service? You've barely spoken to me since I arrived. You're all dark and gloomy and full of self-pity. I don't know what the hell your problem is. I was trying to do something nice for you and all hell broke loose. Pardon me for being kind."

The elevator doors opened and she stepped by him, nose in the air. She steamed down the hallway and stopped outside his suite.

"Go on." He waved at the door. "It's open. I didn't take the time to lock it. You needed me, I came."

She flung the door open and winced when it banged into the wall. She went straight down the hall and slammed her room door. She would not cry in front of him. Not now, not ever. She'd given him everything she had to give. And now, the media would be all over her because she'd been seen with him. How long until they showed up at the inn?

She sighed and dropped against the door, sliding down until her backside was on the floor, her head in her hands. She'd really gone and cooked her goose this time. Silent sobs wracked her body. Going out was a stupid thing to do. She should have waited and asked him how he got groceries. Now, because she'd been impulsive, she was permanently linked to him and he was knocking on *her* door.

"Go away, Brett. I'm busy."

"Steph, please come out. I know the press terrifies you. You—we need to talk about this. Please, honey?"

"Later." Her whisper trembled with tears. She despised herself and her weakness. She reached up and locked the door and crawled over to the bed. She dropped her purse, kicked off her shoes and climbed under the cover and let the tears fall unchecked. "Damn you, Brett Wyatt, why did you stumble into my life?"

It wasn't his fault. Self-pity in the wake of the press attack tore the scab off the wound in her heart, which had never quite healed. She wept until she had no more tears. She stared into nothingness until she drifted to sleep.

It was dark when she awoke, overheated and uncomfortable. A heavy weight draped over her waist and something warm pressed against her spine.

Brett.

How had he gotten into her room and more importantly into her bed without waking her? His arm was limp and unresisting as she moved it off her. He was dead to the world. She stared down at him lying there, shirtless in her bed. She slipped from under the covers and into the bathroom. She closed the door behind her and leaned against the wall. The full-length mirror reflected the afternoon's damage.

Her hair was knotted and filthy, her clothing torn and covered in what looked like coffee and was that jelly? She had a six-inch scratch down one cheek she had no memory of receiving. She must have fought harder than she realized. Good, those jackals deserved it for attacking her again.

She showered and inspected her clothing for damage. Her jeans would survive, but her sweater and T-shirt were little more than rags. She stuffed them into the garbage and slipped out of the bathroom, wrapped in a towel.

Brett sat, bare-chested, in her bed; looking like sin incarnate.

Figures, she was a disaster, he was a god.

"Did the shower help?"

"Not as much as the nap." She felt her smile wobble.

"Come, sit here." He patted the bed. "You have to see this. You made the six o'clock news."

"No." She groaned and covered her face with her hands.

"I think you're going to like this." He slid over and patted the bed again.

"Let me get dressed."

"Pfft. No need. I've seen you naked." He waggled his eyebrows. "And that towel covers more than the outfit you had on this morning."

She perched on the edge of the bed. Brett picked up the remote and flicked on the television. "I recorded the best part."

The television came to life with a shot of the reporters crowding someone. The crowd surged and she pushed through; her groceries dropped and she slammed her fist into the reporter's face. The reporter slumped to the ground and her glasses flew off-screen.

"Oh no!"

"Oh yes!" he crowed. "She deserved it for crowding you. That woman has been an enormous pain in my side since I turned her down when she propositioned me after a concert. Couldn't happen to a nicer person." He held up his hand for a high-five and she obliged weakly. "Thank you. I've wanted to do that for years."

"Um. You're welcome?" She winced.

"Get dressed. I ordered dinner. It'll be here any minute." He turned the TV off, crawled over her, kissing her scraped cheek on his way by. "My little superhero. You're incredible."

His superhero? Should she be insulted or pleased? She shrugged. She'd done what needed doing and there was no sense regretting it now.

They devoured their Chinese food, fighting over the spring rolls and deep-fried wontons as they watched movies from the eighties and laughed at the clothing and hairstyles. Their happiness was false bravado to cover their wounds.

She drifted off mid-movie and woke as he carried her to bed. "Put me down, I can walk."

"I can carry you, we're almost there." He dropped her gently on the bed with a mock groan. "Made it. Barely. For a former Stampede Princess, you've got a great right hook. Get in, Princess Slugger."

She groaned and shed her sweats. In T-shirt and panties, she climbed under the covers. He disrobed and paused. She nodded her agreement and he climbed in beside her. She crawled into his arms, snuggled in and went to sleep. She was still in his embrace in the morning.

CHAPTER 15

Three days after the media assault, Brett let Tucker into the suite. They sat in the living room drinking coffee and eating the cookies Steph had baked that morning.

"I've talked to the reporter, the station and the police. No charges will be pressed. The video clearly shows her grabbing your purse. As far as the police are concerned, that's grounds for self-defense against assault. So, you're free and clear." He sipped his coffee. "How are things otherwise?"

"Good." Brett feigned deep interest in the secrets lingering in the bottom of his coffee cup.

"Crappy," Steph disagreed. "He hasn't talked to me. We spend all day everyday together. He won't talk about the surgery or its after-effects. I know it's not good. But he's as tight-lipped as a Catholic priest after confession. I've about reached my limit. I have an inn to run and I can't spend the rest of my life hanging around hoping he grows up enough to talk to me."

"Ouch." He didn't realize she felt like that. She'd shown no indication of being upset with him; although he should have suspected it. It wasn't right to keep her here when she had a business to run. Shit. He was an ass. "So, go home then."

Great, Wyatt. Piss her off even more. Don't you ever think before you speak?

"So, I came here, fought the media, faced my fear of the public only to be proven I was right to be afraid. I came all this way, faced it all, for you. And you thank me by telling me to go home? Wonderful. Brett Wyatt, you're a colossal ass. I wish you'd never walked into my inn. But if you think you're getting rid of me that easily, you can think again. You're acting like a child. You won't get over this unless you face it." She stood and stared at him, hands on her hips.

Every word struck a nerve until he trembled with the urge to scream back at her. She had no idea what he was going through. None. She was clueless to his agony.

"And before you try and tell me I don't understand, consider this. I lost my entire career and my home when Elijah died. I had to run and hide and restart my life. Nobody will *ever* hire me as a teacher, even though it wasn't my fault. Maybe I didn't lose my superstardom, but you can still play guitar. I don't know how serious your voice damage is because you won't tell me; I expect it is permanent. You still have your charities and if you wanted, you could teach music to kids. Concert singing isn't all you are, it's one piece. I'll grant you it was a big piece, but you still have music." Her voice rose until she was almost screaming at him. He winced.

She paused to breathe deeply; her body trembled visibly. "I'm rebuilding, I'm opening a place for kids to come and heal. I'm not sure how, but I'll be able to teach them—something. I'm working it out. You're not even trying. You're avoiding it with movies, video games and dime novels. You, the man with money to burn and every possible advantage, have crawled into a hole and covered up. Maybe I should toss in a blanket and teddy bear. I'm disappointed in you Brett Wyatt, I thought you were more than a vain, childish, superstar. Is that all you've got?"

She snatched up her coffee cup and stomped into the kitchen, leaving Brett and Tucker staring at the doorway.

"Wow. You really pissed her off. I've never seen her like that."

"Me either. But she's wrong. She doesn't know me, or what I'm going through." He was acting childish, but he couldn't stop the petulance.

"Maybe if you talked to her, she might understand. I didn't come to interfere, but she gave up a lot and risked a lot, to come to you—after you left without a note. How many women would do that? She must have seen something special in you, something worth fighting for, but for the life of me, right now, I can't figure out what it might be." He picked up his cup and stood to stare down at Brett.

He looked like a towering black god, full of hellfire and recriminations.

"You're my friend. She's my friend. I thought you might be good together. That's why I told you to book at the inn. I was wrong. She's way too good for you. You're not even trying to deal with this. You're worried about being a has-been. I've got news for you, my friend, if you go down without a fight, you're a never-was. If you won't fight for yourself—fight for her, fight for your fans. Do you think they want to hear about the Brett Wyatt who gave up at the first sign of a struggle? You rose to fame on a wave of glory with barely a hitch. You're rich and famous, but you're a freaking coward. She's one hundred percent right. You can compose, you can teach. Hell, the doctor said you might even be able to sing and record. All you've lost is screaming fans at concerts. You have everything left to live for."

He pivoted on his heel and stormed from the room.

Brett listened to Tucker say goodbye to Steph and promise to call. Her words were too low to hear. Why were they ganging up on him? How could they not see he'd lost everything? Guilt and doubt worried in the back of his mind. Well, screw the pair of them. With friends like that, who needed enemies?

He paced the living room in agitation. Obviously, she wasn't coming back soon. He stormed into his room and slammed the door. His mother's voice echoed in his head. "Brett Wyatt, you close the door properly or I'll take that guitar away for a week." Great, freaking fabulous. Even his mother was getting in on the act. Well, she wasn't taking his guitar. Nobody would steal his music.

He trudged down the hall, past the kitchen and into the music room. Her door had been open and she wasn't in the kitchen; where had she gone? She wouldn't leave without telling him, would she?

He closed the door behind him. He would not go looking for her. He refused. He'd stay right here in this room that had always soothed his soul and search for the magic that had once lived here. He wandered past his display case, debating which guitar to play. The one he'd been given by Fender for a private concert at the children's hospital? The one he'd received from the parents of a teen struck down by cancer, a boy who'd loved Brett's music? His second or third concert guitar? He passed over all ten of the guitars in the enormous display and reached for his first guitar, the one he'd played for Steph.

He checked it over carefully and discovered two worn strings. With the efficiency of years of practice, he restrung and retuned it. He cleaned and polished it with the special cloths he purchased in bulk. He flipped through his collection of picks, selected a new one and sat down. He played the first song he'd ever written as a teenager; an awful, angst-ridden ballad about a girl who'd never seen fit to look at a geek like him. He chuckled at the primitive, badly aligned music and silly words.

He played it through twice, humming along without risking or straining his voice. It flowed into another and another. He played until his fingers ached and shoulders cramped. His body wanted to quit, but his heart and mind urged him to play. His latest hit merged and morphed into something unfamiliar.

He followed the music's urging into the key of A♭ minor. His playing echoed his confusion and despair, the lamenting tones easing his torment. He paused for a second and flipped on the recorder he kept by his chair. The music rarely spoke to him since Elijah had passed on; he needed to get this down before it fled unrecorded.

Elijah. Stephanie. Thoughts of them were melancholy and yet, they were bright spots in his mind, his playing turned lighter. Music for them. Music without words. He knew the lyrics would come later, they often did. Rarely did the tune and lyrics arrive together.

He played and played until his belabored fingers refused to form another note. He set the guitar aside, switched off the recorder and wept. He'd found his music, but he'd lost his voice. Fate was a cruel mistress. He'd been given so many gifts and had them torn from him.

"Remember me," Elijah's voice whispered in his head, sounding all too real and a bright tune flittered through his mind.

"Damn." He had to get this down. He hurried to the desk and grabbed a pad of staff paper and started scribbling down notes. Page after page followed. When the notes ran dry, he scribbled Elijah's Song at the top of the first page and slid the papers into the drawer. He leaned back and sighed, his heart lighter than it had been since his voice cratered at the Stampede. He smiled, his first real smile in way too long.

Angry female voices filtered through the closed door, jerking him back to reality. He checked his watch, he'd played for four hours straight. He flexed his aching shoulders and fingers and headed toward the fracas.

∽

"I don't care." Steph glared at Lola. "He's busy. He doesn't want to see anyone."

"Oh, he'll see me," Lola purred. "I'm his band manager. I do everything for him." Her tone implied she did more than just band work—a whole lot more.

"I understand that. I'm telling you to leave, and he'll call you. If he hasn't returned your calls, he isn't ready to talk to you. He's been through a rough time, give him time to heal."

"He's a recording superstar. He doesn't have time to waste, or the fans will forget he ever existed. I need to talk to him; and you need to leave. I saw that disaster on the news. What were you thinking? Are you trying to ruin his reputation? The press came to hear about the surgery, not to battle with a little country nobody."

"How did the press learn about the surgery?" Steph demanded. Had Lola told them? The hospital wasn't likely to leak the news and Brett certainly hadn't given a press release.

"That's what I'd like to know." Brett's voice carried a wealth of anger.

"Brett, darling." Lola tottered over on her stiletto heels and threw her arms around his neck. She pressed her lips to his in an enthusiastic kiss. "I missed you, baby."

Steph bit down a gag. Brett swore otherwise, but in this second, she believed the tales Lola had been spinning about her serious relationship with Brett.

Brett disentangled himself from Lola and took three steps backward. "Enough, Lola. I warned you. You and I are not an item and we never will be."

"Brett, baby, you know better. Don't let this trollop mess with your head. She's dangerous to your career." She grabbed his arm pleadingly.

The woman had no pride. She just kept going after Brett. The disgust on his face was both comical and reassuring. Brett was going to have to deal with Lola before she caused any more trouble.

"Did you sic the media on me? On Steph?" He shook off her hand and stepped past her to stand beside Steph.

"Only because you need to be in the spotlight. Fans are demanding new concerts. Your manager, JT, is holed up with her friend at that hick inn. He should be out promoting you, keeping you in the spotlight."

JT was with Penny? Wow. Penny hadn't told her that when they talked. Good for them. Penny deserved some happiness.

"I gave the band, and you, time off. I told JT to keep me out of the papers for a while. I have a lot going on right now."

"Like screwing her?" She scrunched up her face and jabbed a thumb toward Steph.

"Whether or not I'm in a relationship with Steph is none of your business. You'll stop referring to her in any manner. She is none of your concern."

Booya! Steph suppressed a grin. *Give her hell, Brett.*

"When are you holding a press conference? Your fans need you." Lola tapped her toes impatiently.

"When I feel like it. Meanwhile, you're fired. Done. I'll have Tucker pick up my office records and keys. Be sure you're around for it and don't keep anything or I'll see you never work again."

"Come on, Brett. I'll leave her alone. She's not that special. She's barely worth the worry. Let's get rolling on a new tour."

"My career is over. The band is done. And you are fired. Don't make me regret hiring you more than I already do." Thunder filled his words.

Steph's head bobbed back and forth between the two as they sparred. Lola was irritating but seeing Brett this upset and standing up to Lola was fabulous. He was standing up for himself. Hopefully, it meant he'd begun healing.

"But, I need this career. You need me," she wailed.

"I won't be touring again. I won't need stagehands and I certainly won't need a band manager. Call Royce Ballentine. I hear he's looking for a manager and he's always had the hots for you."

"Royce?" Her eyes lit with greed. "Fine. I'll call him. Tell Tucker to call before he shows up."

"Thank you." Brett replied graciously. "Now, I'll take my house keys, as well as my bus and van keys, before you go." She handed them over ungraciously. "And if the press gets wind of this, I'll know who to blame because I haven't told anyone else."

"Except her."

"Goodbye, Lola."

She stomped out of the suite. The door slammed so hard it bounced open and hung half open.

"Ouch." Steph winced and closed and locked the door quietly. "You'll have to call a press conference now. Right?" His sigh cut right through her. He wasn't ready to face the press, anyone could see that; but if he hid and Lola went public about the end of his career, it wouldn't look good.

"Do I have to?" He trudged into the living room and flopped onto the couch like a petulant teenager.

She followed and curled up beside him, her face turned toward him. "You probably should. Want to hash it out with me first? We could talk and then you can set something up, or the other way around."

"I'll call JT, he'll arrange something."

Five minutes later, he dropped his cell phone on the coffee table. "Well, two days from now, nine a.m. That's about the soonest he can get it arranged. We'll have it in the media room at Tucker's office."

"What will you say?" She knew she was pushing, but he needed to be ready. Facing the press with bad news was never easy. "Let's bounce some ideas around. If you want to."

"I don't want to." He sighed and scraped his fingers through his hair and across his unshaven chin.

Suddenly, she didn't want to talk; she wanted to drag him into the bedroom and distract him from his worries in the most pleasant way possible. Her body thrummed with desire. Desire would have to wait.

"Take your time. I've got all night. Of course, if you think too long, you'll have to feed me." She kept her voice light so he'd know she was teasing.

"I'll never give a concert again." Defeat dragged his voice down. His expression brightened. "But I composed today. The music for Elijah's Song. I don't have lyrics yet though."

She clapped her hands. "That's wonderful. I mean the composing is wonderful. I'm so sorry you won't give concerts again." She hugged him close and leaned her head on his shoulder. His uneven breathing shivered through her.

"The doctor says with therapy, I might be able to record again, in short time periods. And I can write music, too."

"You don't think that's enough?" Compassion gripped her heart. She knew, all too well, the agony of losing your dream. She wanted to wrap him in cotton and protect him from the cruel reality of the world.

"It's not enough. I can play. I can compose. Maybe, someday, I can record. But I'll miss performing on stage."

"But, you'll save money on band expenses." She grinned into his chest when her lame joke elicited a chuckle. "And no more hotels."

"True." He went still and quiet. "I'm still angry; but I'm moving toward acceptance. I'll have to find something to replace the concerts."

"I'm so thrilled you composed again; and for Elijah, too. He'd be proud of you." She considered their conversation, rolling ideas around in her head. "If you can record, eventually, is there any reason why you couldn't do a song or two at charity events? I know you loved to do the Alberta Children's Hospital live event every year. You only did two songs and manned the phone lines. I talked to you once."

"You did? You never told me."

"A girl needs her secrets. Why did you think I kept the princess thing secret? Wouldn't want you to get bored." She looked up at him and kissed his bristly chin.

"I don't think you'll ever bore me. But charity events might be an idea. Though only time and the doctor will tell me if it's possible." His voice was a little lighter.

They chatted for hours and ate take-out Italian food. Eventually, late in the evening, they had a written speech for the press conference. They climbed into bed together.

"I'd like you to come to the press conference." His voice was low and tentative.

Jeepers. How could he ask that of her? She closed her eyes and fought for an escape. In the end, she sighed. "Yes. I'll come."

∽

Tucker, JT, Steph and Brett stood together in front of nearly a hundred reporters. Television, radio, newspapers and magazines had all sent representatives. Unless she missed her guess, some of them were prominent entertainment bloggers. There were people from both Nashville and California as well. Some of them must have been here since they had learned of his surgery.

JT stepped to the microphone and the room quieted. "Folks, we're going to make this short and sweet. There won't be a question period, Mr. Wyatt will make a statement. Follow-up queries can be directed to my office." The crowd grumbled loudly. "Or," he interrupted them. "Or, we can cancel this entirely and you can wonder what you missed out on."

Steph hid a smile. Nothing like appealing to their base nature.

"If you'll just keep the noise to a minimum, Mr. Wyatt will speak now."

Brett grabbed Steph's hand and stepped forward. Reluctantly, she went with him.

"Thank you all for coming." He pitched his voice low and hoarse. "Most of you have met Miss Alexander. Many of you have falsely accused her in the death of Elijah Marcus. You should know two things. Elijah was my godson and I can tell you, beyond doubt, Miss Alexander was a hero that day. Elijah's death was a tragic accident that neither I nor Tucker Marcus, his father and my lawyer, blame her for. I'm asking you, politely, to stop harassing her."

The crowd mumbled between themselves and after a moment quieted.

"This next bit is difficult for me." He paused and cleared his throat. He gripped Steph's hand tight enough she thought her bones would break. She squeezed back, offering silent reassurance.

"Recently, after my last concert in Calgary, I underwent surgery to repair my damaged vocal cords. I won't bore you with details. Suffice it to say I pushed myself way too hard for way too long and the damage is unrepairable. I'll never give another concert. To do so would risk permanent damage, potentially leaving me unable to speak. I'm undergoing rehab and hope to resume my recording career when I'm healed."

"You haven't released anything for years," a female shouted.

"True. Elijah's death tore my muse from my chest. My friendship, my relationship with Steph and the loss of my voice has returned the muse to me. I'm eternally grateful to God and the universe that they've seen fit to restore part of this gift to me. I'm working on a new album, though I don't know when I'll be able to record again."

Steph stared at him. Talking about composing wasn't in the script.

"Aren't you angry?" another voice called.

"I am," he stated boldly. "I'm beyond angry. But anger will solve nothing. I'm entering therapy, physical and mental to overcome this. And with this woman, and my friends by my side..." he waved toward JT and Tucker, "I'll be able to get beyond the anger and find a place of peace. Music will always be part of my life; I just have to work out the details. Thank you all for coming."

He pivoted on his heel and strode toward the door behind them, tugging Steph along with them. Tucker entered the small adjoining room, hot on their heels. JT stayed behind to finish things up.

Steph hugged him. "You never told me."

He picked her up and whirled her around in a circle, nearly banging into Tucker. "I never had time. I had the blowout with Lola, we concocted a plan and here we are. I'll play the tunes for you. I'm thrilled to compose again." His face fell. "I'll miss concerts, but I'm trying my damnedest to count my blessings." He turned to Tucker. "I'll get the name of the shrink you told me about. I'm not going to be able to move on without professional help."

"You've got it, friend." Tucker clapped him on the back and they shared a loose man-hug.

JT came into the room laughing. "That was one curious mob out there. I finally got rid of them by promising weekly updates on your condition."

He walked up to Steph. "Are you okay that this numbskull aligned you with his recovery and his life? You looked shell-shocked."

"Um. Ya? No? I have no idea. I'm not sure I can be in the public eye. I detest it."

Brett embraced her. "I'll keep you out of the spotlight as much as I can. But, I do need you by my side." He paused. "Please."

"And my inn? My career?" She shook her head. "I'm not giving up another career. The inn is my life's work. Someday, I'll have something up and running. Something that caters to kids, probably kids and family who've undergone accidents and tragedies. I won't give that up."

"I'm not asking you to. All I'm asking is a few more days. For now. We need time to figure out a few things, especially how we can more forward. Together. I love you, Stephanie Alexander. I know I haven't said it before and my timing sucks. But I fell in love with you when I saw you dancing and heard you butchering my music."

"Your timing super-sucks." She wrinkled her nose at him.

"But you love me, too? Right?"

She threw her arms around his neck and kissed him senseless. "You don't deserve it," she teased. "But, I do love you, Brett Wyatt."

"Come on, JT, let's leave these two lovebirds alone."

"You better believe it. I'm headed back to the ranch to see Penny. Since I don't have a band or career to manage at the moment, I have free time for dating."

CHAPTER 16

Steph answered Brett's door and invited his counsellor, Bev, inside with the realization that being a superstar had its perks. The counsellor had visited Brett's suite for two hours every day for the last week. Most of the time, Steph busied herself away from the music room where they had their sessions. Occasionally, they invited her to join them for part of the discussions.

Brett's mood ran the gamut from the darkest black of despair to the brilliant colors of creation. Steph did her best to hang on for the ride, but she was starting to miss her home and her job. She had clients coming and going and it wasn't fair to leave Penny, and JT, in charge for any longer. She had to leave Brett alone and return to her life.

Bev sat in the armchair; Steph sat beside Brett, on the couch. They were close enough to touch, and the heat of his denim-clad thighs burned into her legs through her light cotton shorts. It was surprisingly difficult not to crawl onto his lap for a hug when he was baring his soul. Reluctantly, she broached the subject of leaving, hoping the counsellor's presence might act as a buffer.

"I don't want you to leave," Brett exclaimed. "We're not done working through this."

"Oh, honey. This is your issue to resolve. I can't find a resolution for you. I love you and I want to help; but I have a life to get back to. I can't put it on hold forever."

"I thought I was part of your life." His brows furrowed and he glared at her.

"You are. Don't ever think you aren't important to me. You're an enormous part of my life and I love you." She caressed his clenched fist, stroking it until it relaxed. "I can't believe how much I love you after such a short time; but, my life and my career are waiting for me."

"Right, kick me when I'm down." He jerked his hand out from under hers.

She was approaching this all wrong and couldn't fathom a better way to attack it. She looked at Bev for insight.

"Brett, are you saying you don't think it's fair for Stephanie to leave you when you're at a low point?"

"That's exactly what I'm damn well saying." He lurched to his feet, stomped to the window and stood with his back toward them. "How can you do this to me?"

"You've undergone a horrible life-altering event. I know exactly what it's like to lose everything. I lost my students, my job, my fiancé, my friends. All I had left was my family and Tucker. You still have all of that. You've got career options, even if you don't want to acknowledge them."

His shoulders tensed and his hands balled into fists. "Easy for you to say."

"Actually, it isn't. Your pain, your agony, hurts me as much, if not more, than what I've gone through." She sucked in a deep breath, fortifying herself and shoring up her courage. "But you're more than a stage presence. You have a charity to help children. The doctor said yesterday that you'll be able to record, just not doing endless concerts. You can play, you can sing. You could teach if you wanted to. The world is your oyster and you're wallowing over one lost pearl. That's a load of bull crap. Complete and total bull crap.

There are seven stages of grief and you refuse to let go of the anger and self-pity. Eventually, you'll have to accept your lot in life and move on."

Oh God, she had to shut up before she said something even worse than she already had. She'd been there, she should know better, but for the life of her, she couldn't stop needling him. Revisited anger over her past fueled her frustration with Brett.

"I love you, but I can't, no I won't, stay any longer. It's not an easy decision for me; but our lives, as they stand now, are irreconcilable. I want more than this. I want to find a place where we can both be happy. The city is stifling me." Her mouth gaped open. Until the words escaped, she hadn't identified the quiet unease she'd been feeling since she had arrived. Her mind had tied it to Brett and his loss, but it wasn't just that. It was her longing for home. She could visit him here, but urban living would crush her.

He seemed to enjoy his time at the ranch, but he'd never declared one way or the other if he could live there. Their time at the ranch had been idyllic, but it was too early to delve into such deep subjects. She wanted to try and continue a relationship, but on terms they were both comfortable with.

"You could come with me. I have my bi-weekly sessions online. You could do the same."

"So, you won't stay with me, but you expect me to move for you? There's some hypocrisy for you."

"I don't believe that's what she meant. Is it?" Bev injected. "Can you reword that? Clarify it for us?"

"I meant I'd like to make this relationship work, I'd like to help you find your way to heal, but I can't ignore my own life. Maybe we could split our time between the two places; once I hire a manager for the inn. I'd have to run some numbers first, and see if I can afford one. Without the income from your stay, I wouldn't be paying for Penny to manage right now." She hated the doubt and insecurity which crept into her voice. Part of her wished she'd taken the easy way out, like he had, and just snuck out in the night; but that wasn't any way to run a friendship, let alone a romance.

He whirled round from the window. "You're asking me to fund your ranch? That's rich."

She gaped at him and snapped her mouth shut. "No! You're being belligerent and deliberately taking my words out of context. The inn supports me, comfortably, but if I dump my income to pay for a manager, I'll have nothing left to live on. I won't live off someone else's hard work. It's not in me to scrounge. I make my own way. I have since I left home to go to university."

Fiery anger and disappointment burned her insides; heat rose in her face. She stood and faced him. "Brett Wyatt, look at me." She cupped his cheeks in her hands and turned his face toward hers. "I love you, more than I've ever loved anyone else. But I won't be beholden to you and I won't give up my dreams for you. I think we can find a compromise—somewhere. I'm not saying it won't be work, because it will. But, you're worth the effort, I just thought you might think I was worth it, too."

She kissed his chin and holding her head high, biting back tears, she walked from the room. She packed her things inside her suitcase with trembling hands and walked back through the living room. He hadn't moved from where she left him.

"Nice to meet you, Bev. Goodbye, Brett. You have my number and you know where I live. When you want to talk, you know where to find me. I hope you find a resolution you can live with."

She paused a moment, giving him a chance to speak. For a second, he looked like he might say something; but he turned his back on her without a word.

She made her way downstairs and into a cab without crying. By the time she reached the airport, she'd cried herself dry. The flight home was tedious and full of turbulence. Headwinds kept them in the air for an extra forty-five minutes. Penny picked her up at the airport and in an hour and a half, she was in her bed, crying herself to sleep.

Damn, stubborn, intractable man!

She got up in the morning, showered, plastered on her game face and met Penny in the kitchen.

"Ready to talk?" Penny hugged her tightly.

"Nothing to say." She sighed. She didn't want to talk about this. Brett Wyatt was nothing but trouble. "I should have gone with my gut. He wasn't the man for me, and I should have stayed away from him no matter how sexy and endearing he is."

"Is or was?" Penny patted her back.

"Is, was, whatever. He's gone. I'm done. I have an inn to run, a career and a life. He's got Toronto and his music. Never the two shall meet. Buttered buns! I feel like I'm stuck in the middle of a B-movie or a Shakespearean tragedy."

"So, you love him then?"

"No!" She'd keep denying it until her heart believed it. Superstars were nothing but a big pain in the—heart. "I could write a song about men's fickle hearts."

"Tell me you didn't give him an ultimatum? Please." Penny moved to the counter and poured two enormous mugs of coffee, topping them off with Baileys and whipped cream.

"A little early for that, isn't it? I'm not planning on drinking my problems away, nor am I going to let him upset me." She waved the mug away.

Penny rammed the mug into her hands, nearly sloshing the hot liquid over the edge. "It's half an ounce. It'll take the edge off so we can talk. No guests until late afternoon. By then the *enormous* amount of booze in that will be long gone. Right now, dish! Tell me everything. Am I going to have to hike to Toronto and kick his jerk ass?"

"Yes. No. I don't know." Indecision ran through her. Had laying down the law been a mistake? Should she have given him more time? "I am such a loser." She sniffed and brushed away a tear. "I should have approached it more softly."

"How did you approach it?" Penny guided her to the table and they sat across from one another, hands wrapped around their mugs, like fingers clutching a life-line.

"I told him to suck it up, I was leaving. The city was killing me and I had a life." She raked her fingers through her hair and fisted the strands against her scalp. A plague of locusts set loose in her stomach and she bit back a gag of sorrow at her own impulsiveness.

"Any chance of taking it back? Or did you totally kill everything?"

"Well, if one fight kills his feelings for me, I made the right decision, didn't I?" Cold dread trickled down her spine in slow motion, like honey on a frigid day. Fiery anger climbed her face until she feared she would ignite. Nothing was what she'd thought it was.

Could she live without him now that she'd found him? Or had she burned the wrong bridge? Self-doubt plagued her. She wasn't the impulsive type but everything about their relationship had been impetuous. Too hot, too fast and over too quick. What was the expression? The fire that burns hottest burns half as long, or something. She'd never been attracted to anyone like she had been to Brett, let alone at first sight. What had she been thinking?

"I wasn't thinking. I was overcome with lust and crazy emotions."

"Like love?" Penny's lips quirked upwards like she was hiding a smile.

"Love, lust; whatever it was I'm over it."

"That's bull-puckey. You're in so deep you can't see your way out. So, you screwed up, got scared and bolted. So-freaking-what? You said it yourself, if he quits after one fight, he's not worth your time or your effort. You deserve better."

"Yes, she does." His voice was stronger than it had been, but not as robust as before the surgery.

Steph jumped to her feet, toppling her mug. It shattered in an explosion of coffee and ceramic shards. "What are you doing here?" she demanded, backing away from the doorway, glaring at Brett.

God, did he have to look so good? What was he doing here?

"I came to talk to you. This isn't over." He pointed his finger back and forth between himself and Steph. "We need to talk. I sure as hell don't know where I'm going in my life, but when you walked out I realized that wherever I went, I wanted you by my side."

"I approached it wrong," she hedged, "but, I meant every word I said."

"I believe you. I like a woman who sticks to her principles."

She edged back when he stepped toward her. Another step, another retreat until her back was pressed against the pantry door. "You're, you're making a mess. You're grinding that mug into the floor."

"I don't give a shit about the mug." He reached forward with his right hand. "I only care about you."

"And your career?" God, when would she learn to keep her mouth shut? She'd just lamented how she'd acted and she was wearing those stupid shoes again.

"My career?" He laughed dourly. "That ship has sailed. Concerts are done. I have to find a new passion." His finger slid down her cheek like a silken ribbon; its cool softness leaving heat in its wake.

"I'm not a new passion." She objected, batting his hand away.

"I didn't mean it like that. I meant, I love you. I need you. I want to spend my life with you. Career decisions can wait until I get my head screwed on straight. I've got money to live fairly comfortably until I know what I want."

"Fairly comfortably?" Penny croaked.

"You. Out." Steph banked a smile when Brett shooed Penny toward the door. "Go away. We'll call you. Later. Much later. Take the day off."

"Steph?"

"You might as well go." She sighed. "I'll clean this up. I'll be fine." Calm certainty settled in her chest, and the pain around her heart lessened.

"What if you guys leave and I clean up?" Penny hurried to the pot and made two more coffees with Baileys and whip cream. "Here, take these. Go away. Go upstairs. I'll handle the mess." She passed them the mugs and stood glaring at Brett. "If you do anything stupid. So help me God, I'll have your balls for bookends."

His wince left no doubt that he believed her. Steph kissed her friend on the cheek. "Thanks, hon. I always could count on you. I'll text if I need you."

"Watch yourself, mister!" Penny's glare elicited thoughts of maiming and loss of vital body parts. He shivered.

"Your friend is safe in my hands. Safer now than she ever was. I promise, on my life and on my genitals."

Penny squinted and he backed out of the mess on the floor. Safe from the glass, he stepped out of his shoes and retreated from the kitchen without turning his back on her. He pulled Steph gently by the hand giving her time to pick her way across the debris.

She really should resist him. He was too charming, too attractive and too manly. Heck, he was just plain too much of everything. Still, he'd come all this way. For her. Her heart twittered with delight.

"How did you get here so fast? I waited hours for a flight." She tugged at his arm, halting his progress up the stairs.

"I hired a private jet. I didn't want you to think I waited too long to come after you." He pulled her forward. "I'd like to talk. In private. In your suite. The sitting area, not the bedroom. Though that'll come later." He pivoted and flashed a smile and a wink.

She rolled her eyes. Men! She unlocked her room and they went inside. She sat in a chair, avoiding the couch and ignoring his 'you-can't-fool-me' look. She leaned back, crossed her arms over her chest and waited—and waited. He paced back and forth across the small room. His shoulders were tense and his forehead wrinkled. He seemed to be struggling with where to begin. Well, she wasn't going to go easy on him. He was a grown man, capable of speaking his mind. She'd wait to hear what he had to say before kicking him out.

It would take some pretty fancy talking to convince her he was sorry and he was ready to sort out his life. She'd brace herself against his pretty face and batten down her hormones.

∽

BRETT PAUSED and looked out the window, struck by the irony that this was entirely too similar to where she'd left him. He needed to get his shit together and make this right.

"I apologize for not being sensitive to your dislike of the city. I was, and I am, wrapped up in my own problems. Honestly, I have no idea how to straighten out my life. This is a lot to swallow for me. My entire life plan is shot to hell. I'm not coping well." He turned away from the window.

She was watching him, her expression neutral, making it hard to read what she was thinking. He'd like more to go on, but he understood her reticence. She'd stood in his place and survived when her career was destroyed. If anyone understood his pain, it was her. He hadn't realized until she walked out that she had more to offer than just friendship and love. She had a deep understanding of his mental anguish.

"I feel—weird," he blurted. *Great, way to make yourself look like a jerk.* "You and I connected so quickly. Half the time I didn't know whether to pull you closer or run for my life."

"Gee, thanks."

"You know exactly what I mean. Sometimes, I could see you thinking the same thing. I didn't realize it, but it's okay to be nervous, to be scared. Though if you ever tell anyone I said that, I'll deny it." He smiled, hoping to break her frozen expression. It almost worked. Her eyes lost some of their ice and his heart melted.

He had to get his freaking thoughts, and words, in order before she kicked him out.

"I don't know where I thought this relationship was headed. Someplace good I think. But those three concerts, one after another —" He swallowed hard, remembering the pain and fear that had overtaken him. "They were too much. If I had listened to the doctor after the first incident, I might not have ruined my voice. I've got nobody to blame but myself."

He trundled around the room, picking things up and setting them back down without looking at them. "Do you have any idea how hard it is to admit my desperate need for approval is what caused my downfall? If I hadn't been so needy, I would have backed off, rested and saved my career. I felt ten-feet-tall and bullet-proof. God, I'm such an idiot."

"Why the desperate need for approval? I don't understand."

"We've talked about this. How my family wanted me to get a 'real job'. Bev taught me a lot during the past week. She called bullshit on every lie I told myself. She helped me realize that no matter how many concerts I gave, I'd never win the approval I'd wanted as a boy. When you walked out, it was like I was cold-cocked. It was an emotional shot to the balls to realize how important you were." Her wince made him rake his fingers through his hair, searching for the right words.

"Watching you walk away brought everything, and I mean *everything*, into focus." He paused to look at her. After a long, tense silence, she spoke.

"And the definition of everything is?"

He nearly laughed. Lord, she was a tough nut to crack. She wasn't going to give him an inch. He loved that side of her. Tough, strong, and independent; but kind, generous and loving, too.

"Where to start? From the past, I guess. I'll never get that approval I wanted from my parents, even with my success and my charity work. It doesn't mean they don't love me. I think they value my charity above my talent and they're probably right. My voice is gone, or almost gone; but I'll do the physio and hope for enough to keep recording on a light schedule."

He dropped onto the couch, elbows on his knees and leaned toward her. "But I'm more than a voice; you gave that to me. Your words hammered that point home. I can play, I can compose, maybe sing and I can teach. I'm not sure which way I'll go, but I'm not going to rush the decision. There's only one decision I'm going to rush." He studied her face and her clenched hands. She wanted to hear him out, that was a good sign. A fabulous sign. He might just save this.

"I want you in my life. That decision is certain, solid and unchanging. I don't know how the hell we'll reconcile this, but I think if we work together, we can find a way to stay together." He dropped to his knees in front of her making her rear back.

"I want to spend the rest of my life with you. I need you to keep me on the straight and narrow, to keep my ego in check and my heart safe. I need you, I want you. I love you! Can you ever forgive me for being an ass?"

He grasped her hands in his and waited. She didn't pull away. Neither did she smile or show any other emotion. *Shit.* He'd ruined it. He'd said the wrong thing. What did women need to hear?

He tried again. "I want to find a happy medium, where you can keep your lifestyle and dreams and I can find a new passion."

"I won't leave the inn," she warned him.

"I don't want you to. I'll sell my condo and buy a place in Calgary. Or Okotoks. Hell, I'll give the neighbor whatever he wants and buy his place. I just want to be with you. I'll even do it before we decide we're a thing."

She laughed, a smile breaking across her face and lighting her beautiful brown eyes. "A thing? That's the best you've got?"

"No, you're the best I've got. At least I hope I've got you. You're everything to me. I'd give up my guitar for you."

"Liar." She stroked his cheek. "You'd never give up music. It's more a part of you than singing in concert. You just haven't figured it out yet. I'd like to see where this relationship goes, to see where it ends up; but I don't expect you to give up your life for me. We can compromise."

"Bad news, baby. I've got my place listed already and movers booked. I'm coming this way. I'm coming after you hard and relentlessly until you realize you love me as much as I love you."

"That's insane!"

"I'm crazy in love with you. I want you to be my wife, to live with me and love me forever." He kissed her knuckles one after the other until his lips had brushed them all.

"I love you too, Brett Wyatt."

"Yes!" He fist-pumped the air and she laughed. "My stuff arrives next week." He grinned his cockiest grin.

"Pretty confident, aren't you?"

"Hell no. I was certain you'd kick me out on my ass the second I walked in. But I'm risking everything, willingly, to be near you. I'll hammer at your defenses until you cave in and marry me."

"Is that some kind of backhanded proposal?"

Shock ricocheted down his spine. Certainty and happiness followed right after, warming his body and his heart. "No." He regretted his answer when her smile fell.

He pulled her hands to his chest. "Stephanie Alexander, I'm nothing without you. You're my everything. My heart and my soul. Will you do me the honor of being my wife? Please. I promise to help you follow your dreams and not be too big of an ass."

She raised one eyebrow. "You had me for a minute." She laughed. "Yes, Brett Wyatt. I will marry you. I'll even let you live in my castle until you grow up and find your dream."

"That was a low blow." His heart skipped with joy. "But I'll take that offer. I'll need a recording studio and a music room."

"Buy it yourself, you've got enough money." Her laughter flooded him with warmth. He pulled her into his arms and they tumbled on the floor together in a tangle of limbs, their lips meting in a promise to each other.

"I love you, Steph." He trailed kisses down her silken neck to the collar of her T-shirt.

"I love you back."

"Just my back?" He laughed, light happiness filling every pore.

"Well, your front might have its positive attributes."

Her lips were like molten heat on his neck and chest. "I think we should move this to the bedroom." He panted.

"Ha. What makes you think you're getting any?"

"I'm the man, and I'm the boss of you." He scooped her into his arms and carried her to the bedroom. He dropped her on the bed and smiled down at her. Surely, she could see the love in his eyes.

"Just because you can toss me around, doesn't mean you're the boss of me."

Her gaze met his and his heart stuttered. "No, you'll always be in control. I'm weak and helpless without you. Together, we make each other whole. May I please join you?" She opened her arms and welcomed him home. "We'll sort out the logistics later," he whispered against her neck. "Together."

CHAPTER 17

The next few days passed in blissful reunion. They rode quads all morning so she could familiarize him with the ranch boundaries and the staff. They helped deliver a late calf; she vowed to determine how a cow had been bred so late in the season. "Okay, mercy," she pleaded. "I need sustenance. You've kept me holed up in this bedroom for days. I'm ravenous."

"I have not. You've worked and ignored me while you did so. I was forced to talk to my shrink and play my guitar. Alone." He made his voice warble and she laughed.

"Yeah, but I'm hungry now! It's lunch time. I don't have guests today, but I do need to eat or I'll wither away."

She kissed him deeply; their lips clashing a loud growl from her stomach put them back on track and they wandered to the kitchen for lunch.

"About time you guys surfaced," Tucker teased.

Steph threw herself into her friend's arms. "Tucker, what are you doing here?"

"I came to check on pretty-boy." He pointed his thumb at Brett. "He isn't answering his phone or returning my texts. I thought you might have buried him out in the yard." He chuckled deeply. "He would deserve it."

"Get over yourself, Tucker." Brett laughed.

"He's okay. He needs training, like a bad dog." Steph laughed. "But I think I can straighten him out."

Brett glanced around the room. Penny sat on JT's lap with her arm slung around his shoulder, ever-present coffee cup in her hand.

"Morning, Penny. JT. Is this an intervention?" Brett asked, half-serious. "If it is, you forgot to invite my parents."

"Yes. And no." Tucker laughed and scratched his bald head.

"Can you clarify that?" Brett glanced at Steph. Her shrug told him she was as clueless as he was.

"It's not an intervention. But, we've put our heads together and we might have an idea. And we did invite your parents." JT laughed.

"What?" Brett took a half-step back.

"Hi, Brett."

Brett whirled around to face the familiar voice. His mother, impeccably groomed as always stood beside his father. They smiled tentatively.

"Mom? Dad?"

"We came to see you." His mother stepped toward him, hand outstretched as if to embrace him.

"Why? We haven't seen each other in months. Why now?"

"Because, we realize what losing your career must have cost you," his dad offered and turned toward Steph. "You must be Stephanie. I'm Brett's father, Ryan and this is my wife, Sheila. It's nice to meet the woman who captured our son's heart."

"Nice to meet you both. I'm Stephanie Alexander. Welcome to the Wild Rose Inn. Can I get you anything?"

Brett wanted to puke. How could she be nice to them? She knew they hated his career. She should be supporting him. He didn't need this. He was just finding his way back to a degree of happiness and they had to show up and ruin everything.

"We're fine, Stephanie." Sheila turned to face Brett. "We've been talking with Tucker and we'd like to help."

"I'm sure you would. I'm sure nothing would please you more than helping me find a more suitable career. I'm done." Why now? Where had they been in the early days of his career when he had struggled. They'd been so busy pushing him toward law, medicine, accounting, anything but music. They'd missed his passion. Now they show up? He backed toward the door.

"Brett, wait." Steph placed her hand on his arm. "Don't you think you should talk about this? You chose not to see your parents in Toronto, and they came a long way to see you."

Crap, he'd have to stay or look bad in front of his future wife. "Fine. Talk." To his surprise, his father ignored his rude attitude and started speaking.

"We've made a lot of mistakes. Too many to count. We wanted more for you than playing in a bar band."

"It was hardly a bar band." Brett rolled his eyes. Steph sighed loudly.

"You're right." His mother jumped in. "It was considerably more than a bar band. Overnight you turned from an entry level opening act to a mega-star. By then, the rift between us was a chasm too big to cross. We didn't know how to approach you and you never came home." His mother's voice wavered. "I wanted to tell you how proud I was of you, of your career, and your success. But I was a stubborn fool and didn't want to risk being pushed away." Tears rolled down her face and Steph handed her a tissue.

"So now you're here. Why?"

"Brett!" Steph's admonishment knifed guilt through him. Okay, maybe he wasn't helping things. He raked a hand through his hair.

"Sorry. I'm on edge."

"Your mother and I talked to Tucker; a lot. We helped come up with a plan. You might not like our interference, or our plan, but it's something to consider going forward."

"A plan for what?" Discomfort rolled in his stomach like dogs fighting over a bone.

"For your future," Penny piped in with a grin. "Me, JT, Tucker and your folks talked. A lot. We had a flash of inspiration. You're gonna like this!" She shifted excitedly on JT's lap.

"Stop moving, wiggle pants. You'll fall off my lap and spill your coffee," JT chided her with a laugh. He wrapped his arm around her waist and pulled her close.

"I think I'll need coffee and breakfast to make this palatable." Brett groaned. With them all ganging up on him, he had no option but to hear them out.

Steph rummaged in the fridge. "I'm making omelets. Anyone interested?"

Brett leaned uncomfortably against the wall. Regrets and recriminations rolled around in his head. Had he been so stubborn his own family wouldn't risk talking to him? Was he completely unapproachable? Sure, he'd been busy, and the few family gatherings they'd had were noisy affairs and he was often arriving late and leaving early. Half of the fault was his.

"Mom, Dad, I'm sorry if I was unavailable. I should have tried to talk to you about my dreams instead of cutting you out. I was hurt that you supported everyone's dream but mine. I refused to come to you and talk about it."

"Oh, Brett." His mom rushed over to embrace him. "We were no better, we've been stuck in our opinions. Let's move past that now."

His father offered his hand. Brett shook it and pulled him into a man-hug. "Thank you, both of you, for coming to help."

∼

STEPH AND PENNY whipped up breakfast and everyone sat down in the dining room to eat, a carafe of coffee ready for refills.

"So, tell us about this great idea." Steph looked from one to the other, not certain she really wanted to hear it. She smiled at Brett's parents, and pinned Tucker with a glare. "Why do I think you're the instigator in this?"

He grinned unrepentantly. "Because I am." He ate a few bites and set his fork down. "We knew you guys would end up together. Any idiot could see that, despite the bumpy road you shared. We're tickled pink. You're well suited to one another. I have to be honest. I worried you might not resolve your differences if Brett kept touring. So, in a way, Brett's damaged vocal cords are a blessing in disguise."

"Are you freaking insane?" Brett blurted. His fork clattered to his plate.

"Hear us out. Don't get your shorts in a twist just yet." Tucker's laugh reverberated off the walls. "Brett's folks didn't come in until later, when we decided to feel them out about the idea." He swallowed some coffee and continued. "Steph wants to stay on the ranch. She wants to run some kind of charity or open the ranch up to kids somehow. Brett runs a children's charity and has money to burn. I've got the legal knowledge. Penny's an amazing cook and JT has a teaching degree in elementary education." He paused dramatically.

Steph's heart sped up. She could see where this was going. It could work.

"So, we form a charity to help sick or injured kids and their families. We have them out to the ranch for healing. JT will teach. Penny will cook. I'll help with the ranching and be the manager and deal with permitting and such."

"What am I, just a money tree you pluck when you need more cash?" He didn't sound bitter, he sounded excited.

"Not at all!" Penny shifted in excitement. "You can teach music. You play guitar and piano, you've got a lot to give. We'll hire a voice teacher to help out."

"A year-round retreat where they can heal their bodies and spirits without losing pace with their education." Steph clapped her hands, excitement poured through her and she leaped to her feet. "This is exactly, I mean exactly, what I was thinking of. A place for children and their families to heal after illness. I just hadn't put my finger on it. There are so many details to work out." She paced the room spouting ideas as she went. "We'll need more housing, classrooms, musical instruments, home schooling programs, more staff —" She trailed off. She couldn't even formulate all the details

She whirled round to face Brett. "Oh, we're asking a lot of you. Do you want to do this? Could you even consider it?" She placed her hand on his shoulder. It tensed up under her light touch. His mouth turned down for a moment and his brows creased.

"You've always been great with kids, Brett," his mother said. "I thought I'd have dozens of grandkids by now." She winked at Stephanie.

Grandkids? Was she nuts? They weren't even married yet.

Steph looked at Brett's frown. Crap. He didn't like the idea. Was teaching beyond what he felt he could do?

"I don't know—oh, what the hell. I can play and teach. I'm in if I create a recording studio we can use for me and for the students." He wrapped Steph in his arms, stood and whirled her around until she was dizzy. "I don't think I'm jumping into this too fast, it feels right, it feels like the perfect solution. Are you in, Penny? JT? I can tell Tucker's all in by his big, stupid grin."

"Yes!" Everyone agreed in unison.

"You know," Brett's father spoke. "Brett can stay in the public eye and be the face of the charity. His celebrity will do more than all the advertising in the world."

"Perfect." JT grinned. "Frankly, I was getting tired of the touring. I'll be glad to put my teaching degree to work. I'm not sure how I ended up being a band manager to begin with."

"Because you're the most organized person I know. With you running the business side and Lola managing the crew, I had all the organization I needed." Brett sat down, Steph on his lap. "This is going to work. I can feel it way down deep."

Brett hugged her close and leaned his head against hers. "Mom, Dad, you should know Steph and I are getting married. Soon."

His mother stood and rushed over to them. She hugged them tightly, squishing Steph's breath right out of her. "Darling, welcome to the family!"

Somehow, Steph knew she was including Brett in her enthusiasm.

"Um. Thank you. I adore your son. But, don't get your hopes up on those grandkids."

"Yet." Brett laughed.

Jeepers, they hadn't discussed anything yet and Brett was promising his mother kids? Her heart blossomed. She could live with that. Oh yeah, she'd love to have Brett Wyatt's babies.

CHAPTER 18

First Saturday of Stampede. Two Years Later.

Steph rolled over in bed to hug her husband. Today was a double blessing. It marked one year of wedded bliss to Brett. Equally as important, today they welcomed their first family to the ranch. Tommy and his mother, the family who had been at Brett's last concert were coming. Tommy had finished his latest round of chemo and needed a safe place to rest.

Brett tugged Steph into his embrace and nuzzled her neck. "I suppose we should get up." He slid lower on the bed, his morning stubble scraping playfully against her skin.

"Mm. I think not." She gripped his shoulders and pulled him up. "I need some kisses."

"As my lady wishes." His lips brushed softly against hers and she sighed in delight.

"Or maybe, I need to kiss you." She rolled him onto his back and straddled him, pinning his arms over his head. She grinned at him. "Good morning, Mr. Wyatt."

"Good morning, Mrs.—"

She interrupted him by taking his mouth with hers. "No more

talking," she whispered against his lips. "Love now. Talk later." She inched lower trailing kisses on his chest and abdomen.

Twenty minutes later someone pounded on their door. "You guys up yet?" Penny hollered. "Brett, you've got things to do. Steph, I need you downstairs."

"Coming, Brett shouted. "Whew, we finished that just in time." He chuckled and tickled her neck. "I need your help in the studio for a few minutes. Can you spare me ten minutes before you start work?"

She groaned. "Gah. I suppose. If I must." Her words dripped mock reluctance. "But I get to shower first."

"I'll join you."

Cold air washed over her when he flipped the covers off.

"No, you will not join me. If you do, it'll be another hour before we get out of this suite. Go. Shower in a guest room. Your old room is empty. Just let Penny know which one you used so it gets tidied up later." She scooted off the bed. "Meet you in the kitchen in fifteen minutes." She bolted into the bathroom, locking the door behind her.

∼

"So, what do you need help with?" she asked as he led her into his recording studio.

"Can you sit?" He pointed toward a comfortable-looking chair big enough for two people to curl up in.

"O-kay." She studied him from head to toe. He was tense and nervous. Clenched hands, raised shoulders and shifting feet. She settled into the chair without further comment.

He set a folding chair in front of her and pulled his first guitar from its display case. "This isn't easy for me," he stated and settled across from her, guitar in his lap. "I'm baring my soul here."

She reached out and caressed his hand. "Your soul is safe with me; as is your heart, my dear husband. Play for me."

Indecision crossed his face, followed by fear and then determination.

He tuned the guitar and started playing. "I got the go-ahead to sing again when I went to the doctor last week." He grinned up at her.

"Hooray! You never told me," she chided lightly.

"I wanted it to be a surprise. Recovery took so much longer than we thought. But I made it through. No more rehab and I can sing, carefully, a little each day." He fell silent and focused all his attention on the guitar.

He played and sang a song. Joyful, sad, melancholy and yet full of sunshine. A song about a boy. He never named the boy, but she recognized it as Elijah's Song. Tears of joy ran down her face and she bit back a sob. Poignant and beautiful, the song was certain to be a hit. His fingers stilled but he didn't look up.

She leaped out of the chair and threw her arms around him. "That was incredible." She sniffed. "Beautiful. Has Tucker heard it? Are you going to record it?"

"He hasn't heard it and I don't know yet. I might."

She clapped her hands together. "You must! It's incredible. Thank you for sharing it with me." She showered his face with kisses until they were both breathless.

"I'm not finished," he whispered.

She climbed into her chair and folded her hands in her lap as he started to play a song about a stubborn, lonely, broken-hearted man and the woman who saved him from himself. It was, in a lot of ways, the typical country music feel-good song. But it was more than that, it was an ode to joy and peace, underwritten by love and contentment.

She knew, in her heart, the song was written for her, about her. And she knew it would be a bigger hit than Laughing Heart.

She dropped to her knees in front of him and removed the guitar from his trembling fingers. "Those are the most beautiful words I've ever heard. Both songs. I'm thrilled you found your muse again."

"You're my muse." He looked down and then grinned at her. "You've healed me, even the parts I never knew were broken."

His lips brushed across hers, tasting, caressing, loving her.

"There's more. For another day. An entire album." He paused. "There's a song, not quite finished, about a man and his reconciliation with his estranged family. My family and I weren't estranged, exactly, but we're coming together, with Bev's help. That song, I think I'll call it Broken, is the title track for the album after this one."

"Brett, that's incredible. I had no idea—" She trailed off.

"How could you? But, really, what did you think I was doing all day while you were busy with the inn? I wasn't playing tiddlywinks." He laughed.

"Supervising construction? Riding horses? Checking fences? You do a million things around here. You're a good man and an even better husband." She kissed him again, her heart swelling with love.

"And you are the best wife a man could ask for. But, if we don't hurry, we'll miss Tommy's arrival. We shouldn't ignore our first family."

She leaned into him as they walked to the main house. "Do you think we can do this? Run an inn, a ranch and a sick children's retreat?"

"Laughing Heart Ranch is going to be the best thing this province has seen in years. We're already booking six months out." He cuddled her to his side. "Our friends found us the perfect solution to all our problems."

She laughed and looked up at him, knowing her love glowed like a beacon. "I love you." She stood on tiptoes and kissed him until they were both breathless. As they turned toward the house, again, she asked him, "Do you think Penny and JT will ever tie the knot?"

Brett laughed. "Like you and I, their marriage is inevitable… once they stop trying to avoid it. Maybe they'll get married next year during Stampede. Wouldn't that be something?"

Love the novel you just read?
Your opinion matters.

Review this book on your favorite book site, review site, blog, or your own social media properties, and share your opinion with other readers. Reviews are an author's life blood. To thank readers generous enough to leave a review, I hold a monthly draw for a free e-book. To enter, simply email me the link to your review.

katieoconnorwrites@gmail.com

Each month's winner will receive an e-book
of their choice from Katie's publications.

Thank you in advance, Katie.

WOMEN OF STAMPEDE SERIES

Saddle up for the ride! The Women of Stampede will lasso your hearts! If you love romance novels with a western flair, look no further than the Women of Stampede Series. Authors from Calgary, Red Deer, Edmonton and other parts of the province have teamed up to create seven contemporary romance novels loosely themed around The Greatest Outdoor Show on Earth… the Calgary Stampede. Among our heroes and heroines, you'll fall in love with innkeepers, country singers, rodeo stars, barrel racers, chuckwagon drivers, trick riders, Russian Cossack riders, western-wear designers and bareback riders. And we can't forget our oil executives, corporate planners, mechanics, nursing students and executive chefs. We have broken hearts, broken bodies, and broken spirits to mend, along with downed fences and shattered relationships. Big city lights. Small town nights. And a fabulous blend of city dwellers and country folk for your reading pleasure. Best of all, hearts are swelling with love, looking for Mr. or Miss Right and a happily ever after ending. Seven fabulous books from seven fabulous authors featuring a loosely connected theme - The Calgary Stampede.

WOMEN OF STAMPEDE BOOKS

Hearts in the Spotlight, Katie O'Connor
The Half Mile of Baby Blue, Shelley Kassian
Saddle a Dream, Brenda Sinclair
Eden's Charm, C.G. Furst
Unbridled Steele, Nicole Roy
Betting on Second Chances, Alyssa Linn Palmer
Trick of the Heart, Maeve Buchanan

ABOUT KATIE O'CONNOR

Katie O'Connor lives in Calgary, Alberta, Canada. She married her high school sweetheart and is living her happily ever after. She is the mother of two grown daughters and is extremely proud of her five grandchildren. She has two wonderful sons-in-law and a large support network of friends, family and fellow authors.

Katie's career path has been long and twisted, with most of her life devoted to her family. She's been a waitress, chambermaid, cashier, store manager, as well as a lab and x-ray technician. She is an avid quilter and crafter.

She's dabbled in writing since high school because something drives her to create stories. She swears that it's impossible for her NOT to write. Unsatisfied with one genre, Katie writes contemporary romance, erotic romance and erotica. Recently, she's crafted her first cozy mystery with the intention of publishing a cozy mystery series.

She believes in all things magical; including dragons, fairies, UFOs, ghosts, and house pixies. But most of all she believes in love, romance and hope.

Katie likes to make it up as she goes along and dreams of publishing a mixed genre novel. It is going to be an erotic, shape shifter, vampire, steampunk, sci-fi, murder mystery, adventure, romantic, western, historical, thriller. It will be her biography.

CONTACT KATIE O'CONNOR

Katie loves to hear from her readers.
Feel free to contact her anytime.

Website: https://katieohwrites.com
Email: katieoconnorwrites@gmail.com

Facebook Reader Group: Katie's Kittens:
https://www.facebook.com/groups/345891595596122/

facebook.com/katieohwrites

twitter.com/katieohwrites

instagram.com/katieohwrites

amazon.com/author/katieoconnor

goodreads.com/KatieOConnor

Made in the USA
Columbia, SC
18 May 2018